"What are you doing?"

She'd kicked off her shoes and was beginning to take off her dungarees. Stopped at his question. "Undressing."

"Undressing."

"How else are we going to get cleaned up?"

His mouth opened and closed like he was mouthing the words to a song he knew by heart. He shifted his weight. Put his hands on his hips. Dropped them. Ran a hand over his head.

And she got it.

He was nervous.

"I'm not trying to seduce you," she said with a soft smile. "We really do need to get cleaned up."

"I didn't think you were purposefully seducing me," he answered darkly. "And I didn't say I didn't like it."

Electricity charged the air.

For a brief moment, she considered electrocution.

But they'd been ignoring their chemistry for a reason since the night she'd fallen asleep at his house. They were working together. Stakes were high enough to put their personal feelings aside. More importantly, they didn't want to spoil their friendship...

Dear Reader,

South Africa truly is the most beautiful place I know. I am, of course, biased. I've been surrounded by gorgeous mountains, idyllic beaches and breathtaking vineyards all my life. By setting my books here, I hope to give you all a taste of a part of the world you might not get to see and a glimpse into the settings that inspire many of the scenes in my books.

I cheated slightly with Penguin Island, but I assure you, it's all for you. ;-) The fictional setting of Morgan and Elliott's story is an amalgamation of many different places. Using Boulders Beach as a foundation, one of the only places in the world where you can see the African penguin, I built a paradise that didn't at all help my characters' insistence on not falling in love.

The quaint small town of Penguin Island, with its waterfall hideaways and private beaches, is based on real places scattered throughout South Africa. If you can't make it here someday, I hope through this book you'll be able to experience the beauty of my country.

And, as always, the joy and hope of two people finding their forever with each other.

Happy reading!

Therese x

Finding Forever on Their Island Paradise

Therese Beharrie

Recycling programs
for this product may
not exist in your area.

ISBN-13: 978-1-335-40706-1

Finding Forever on Their Island Paradise

Copyright © 2022 by Therese Beharrie

This edition published by arrangement with Harlequin Books S.A.

For questions and comments about the quality of this book, please contact us at CustomerService@Harlequin.com.

Harlequin Enterprises ULC
22 Adelaide St. West, 41st Floor
Toronto, Ontario M5H 4E3, Canada
www.Harlequin.com

Printed in U.S.A.

Being an author has always been **Therese Beharrie**'s dream. But it was only when the corporate world loomed during her final year at university that she realized how soon she wanted that dream to become a reality. So she got serious about her writing, and now she writes the kind of books she wants to see in the world, featuring people who look like her, for a living. When she's not writing, she's spending time with her husband and dogs in Cape Town, South Africa. She admits that this is a perfect life and is grateful for it.

Books by Therese Beharrie

Harlequin Romance

Billionaires for Heiresses

Second Chance with Her Billionaire
From Heiress to Mom

Tempted by the Billionaire Next Door
Surprise Baby, Second Chance
Her Festive Flirtation
Island Fling with the Tycoon
Her Twin Baby Secret
Marrying His Runaway Heiress
His Princess by Christmas
Awakened by the CEO's Kiss

Visit the Author Profile page at Harlequin.com.

For my husband, who's always given me
the gift of love.

For my sons:

You are, and forever will be, enough.

And for my readers:

Please remember that you are always,
always worthy.

Praise for
Therese Beharrie

CHAPTER ONE

'LIFT YOUR JAW off the floor, darling,' Morgan Simeon's grandmother said in a clipped tone. 'It won't help us if he thinks you're attracted to him.'

'I'm not—'

But Edna had already turned, disappearing into the house at a faster pace than most seventy-year-olds. Edna had been an athlete for years, and her training hadn't stopped when she'd had kids or grown older. Maybe that had been for this very reason. Edna wanted to run away from her granddaughter after a snarky remark, leaving said granddaughter to deal with a millionaire tycoon who held the fate of a very special wedding in his hands.

Shaking her head, Morgan focused on the millionaire tycoon.

She'd been taken aback the first time she'd seen Elliott Abel. That had been a week ago, when her grandmother had first called Morgan for help. Pictures on the internet had shown her how attractive Elliott was. As were all the many women she'd seen pictured on his arm.

Not that that was relevant.

She didn't know why she'd expected him to be unattractive. Perhaps because she'd seen the headlines on those news articles written about him before she'd seen him.

Furniture Tycoon Expands 'Crafted' Empire!
Elliott Abel: The 'Crafted' Furniture Man
From Furniture to Millionaire: the Story of
the Everyday 'Crafted' Man

They'd really honed in on the furniture thing, which made it seem as if there was nothing else interesting about him. And then she'd seen his picture and wondered why the hell journalists neglected to mention that he was a *hot* furniture man.

Much hotter in person.

Now he stood at the end of the path leading to her grandmother's house. Fitted blue jeans, a white T-shirt and matching sneakers adorned his beautiful body. He had a broad chest and shoulders; sculpted biceps; a narrow torso; thick, muscular thighs; and feet that were probably just as attractive.

She'd seen picture of him in suits, tuxedos, but never this casual. Never this…*normal*. He seemed out of place, yet he was clearly comfortable. If her grandmother had stayed long enough for Morgan to reply, that was what Morgan would have told her.

She hadn't been staring because she thought him attractive—well, yes, she did, but that didn't matter. She hadn't done anything about finding someone attractive in ages, and she wasn't going to start with the man threatening to ruin her grandmother's wedding.

No, she had been staring because he seemed so ordinary. But she wouldn't be fooled into believing that.

'Mr Abel,' Morgan said, moving forward. 'Thank you for meeting with me.'

His gaze fell on her almost lazily. 'I thought I was meeting Edna.'

His voice was deeper than she'd expected. It didn't fit the casual look of him. Seemed more appropriate to the bespoke suits of the best quality she'd seen in those pictures.

'I'm Morgan Simeon. Edna's granddaughter.'

'Cavalry.'

It wasn't a question.

'Yes,' she replied softly. 'And you'll find that I'm a much fiercer opponent than she.'

His eyes went dark and there was a flicker of... *something* in their gold and green depths. 'Your grandmother and her friends have been giving me a hard time from the moment I arrived on the island.'

'Only because you're threatening her wedding.'

'No,' he said sharply. 'Not threatening her wedding. Doing the job I was asked to do.'

And there it was. The confirmation to her suspicions.

Elliott Abel, the 'Crafted' Furniture Man, was not the 'son' in Abel and Son Development. That had been clear from her research. But Morgan hadn't been able to find out whether Elliott was still invested in his father's business. Apparently not. He wanted to do what he'd been asked to do and leave as soon as possible.

She could help him with that.

'Your job will go much quicker if you allow my grandmother to get married at the estate before you start development.'

'How would delaying construction by a month make things go quicker?'

'You'd have fewer obstacles.'

'Obstacles have never stopped me before.'

A light shiver went down her spine. A warning, she thought. This man was used to getting what he wanted.

It wasn't the first time she had dealt with someone like him. The people who hired her were often drunk on their own power. And by power she meant money. Heaps and heaps of money that made her clients accustomed to the kind of life she would never understand. Including treating those with less money as if they had less value.

'They will now,' she assured him. 'The people here love me. They love my grandmother even more. If we ask them to co-operate with you, they will. And if we don't...' She shrugged.

He narrowed his eyes. 'What are you saying?'

'I'm saying that if you plan on developing an estate you'll need construction workers.' She lifted a finger. 'People at the harbour to help bring materials onto the island.' Another finger. 'Your general day-to-day needs covered: coffee, food...the same for your workers.' A third, fourth and fifth finger. 'Not to mention the co-operation of the people who are refusing to move out of the estate.'

'Everyone's signed their agreements,' he said tightly. 'Most people have already moved out.'

'Enough people for you to get started,' she agreed, 'but not enough for you to finish. I can think of at least four people who haven't even moved their stuff yet.'

'Your grandmother and her friends.'

'Hmm...' She shoved her hands into her pockets. 'So—a month?'

He didn't respond for a while. When he did, his tone was low, easy. But that shiver went down Morgan's spine again and she braced herself for his rebuttal.

'I see why your grandmother recruited you. You're cunning.' He angled his head slightly. 'But if I allow this you'll ask for more. Maybe

Edna and her friends will want to remain in their houses. Maybe others will. In the end, we won't rebuild, and you'll get everything you want.'

'Wow. The furniture business must be much more cutthroat than I thought if that's what you think.'

He lifted his eyebrows but didn't comment on the fact that she knew who he was.

'I'm not looking to cheat you, Mr Abel. My grandmother has been planning her wedding for the past year—well before your father announced his intentions for the estate. She only wants a chance to see those plans come to fruition.'

She deserved to, too. After Morgan's grandfather had died Edna had been crushed. She'd moved to Penguin Island to get away from memories that hurt too much. The move had been meant to be temporary, but Edna had fallen in love with the island. She had worked through her grief, made new friends, and five years ago had met a man she wanted to spend the rest of her life with.

Morgan had been young when her grandfather had died, so she didn't remember him much. But she did remember the summers she'd come to Penguin Island. Her grandmother had taken care of her and her sister and brother, and for a while Morgan hadn't had to worry about them or her parents. More often than not her parents had gone on their own vacations during those times.

When they'd returned, they'd been happier, and there had been more laughter and affection in her house than before.

She owed her grandmother a lot for that reprieve. For helping to create the happiest memories of her childhood. She would do anything to give Edna a measure of that happiness, even if it meant going toe-to-toe with a tycoon.

'You mean that,' Elliott stated, his eyes searching her face.

'I do. And I'd be happy to sign something to that effect.'

Elliott folded his arms. She tried not to notice the way his biceps bulged under his T-shirt. Instead, she focused on the fact that *this* was the millionaire tycoon she'd been expecting. Not normal or casual, but a man with folded arms, a knitted brow, and beautiful features drawn into hard lines.

Beautiful features?

She ignored that.

'Delaying things by a month doesn't work for me,' he said, his deep voice almost a rumble. 'I promised I'd ensure things move along smoothly. Delaying is not smooth.'

'Things are delayed with developments all the time.'

'Not in my experience.'

'Which is limited, isn't it?'

His lips thinned. 'Yours isn't?'

'No, actually. I work with property developers all the time.' She turned, taking in the estate. 'In fact, I intend on making sure all the houses look presentable for my grandmother's wedding. The videographer is—' She stopped when she realised he wouldn't care. 'Look, the houses here can be repaired. Some need more work than others, but they have good bones.'

'The experts on our team believe differently.'

'Because it's in their interest to do so. And to tell your father—a man with ample money, I'm assuming—that he'll have to knock things down and rebuild them to be profitable.'

'You don't think so?'

'No.' She paused. 'And I think the work I want to do will go a long to making your work easier.'

'You want to renovate these houses before the wedding?'

She laughed. 'Heavens, no. Although I absolutely could. No,' she said again, with a shake of her head. 'I just want the outside of them to look good. If they do, we can take a couple of pictures, put them online, and get some interest for when the estate is ready for…whatever it is you're planning.'

And to tie her entire proposal up with a neat little bow, she smiled.

Elliott blinked.

Morgan Simeon… He still couldn't get the way

she'd said her name out of his head. A husky little whisper that had made him feel inappropriate things. And the smile turned her from a moderately attractive woman into a knockout.

No, that wasn't true. There was nothing 'moderate' about her. And it had nothing to do with how she looked.

It was her confidence. Her shrewdness. This woman who'd arranged a meeting under her grandmother's name had come prepared with a plan that would get her exactly what she wanted. She was the type to always know what she was doing. She was smart, she had a killer smile, and was playing him like a fiddle.

He didn't like it—even though parts of his body had taken an uncomfortable interest in her.

'You're good,' he said. 'Better than your grandmother. That's not an insult,' he added, when her spine straightened.

'It sounded like one.'

'Your grandmother made it personal. You've realised it's business.'

Her smile didn't fade, but her brown eyes, so open before, went sharp. 'Is it?'

There was that shrewdness again. It hit him harder than it should have because he hadn't expected it. She'd obviously looked him up. Knew that the company was his father's and his brother's and that he wasn't a part of it.

Something twisted in his gut, but he ignored

it. Easily. After all, he'd been ignoring that twist for a long, long time.

He took a small breath, keeping his gaze on her, because he had a suspicion she'd seen the inhalation for what it was. An attempt at controlling his emotions. An indication of his irritation at her having the upper hand before he'd even arrived. His frustration that he'd been playing catch-up throughout their conversation. His anger that his brother Gio had asked him to take control of this project when he *knew* this wasn't Elliott's area of expertise.

Now Morgan seemed to know it, too.

He didn't know what he disliked more: the fact that he felt so lost, or that this woman knew it and was using it to her advantage.

There was a shimmer of respect beneath his emotions, he could admit. People rarely went head-to-head with him these days. It was one of the perils of being the person in charge. He had his trusted circle at work. People who would tell him the truth. But even they tried to present honesty softly.

'Elliott, have you considered that perhaps the warehouse isn't coping with orders because of our delivery guarantee? Some items take longer than others. It's just not feasible to have such a short timeframe with the number of orders we get.'

That had been the most recent issue Karlene,

his COO, had brought to his attention. She'd been with him since the inception of his company—well, his empire now, he supposed. They'd expanded into most of Africa already, and turnover was ten times more than it had been when they'd first started making a profit.

Who would have thought that custom furniture made of high-quality material and sold at relatively affordable rates would become so successful? He'd hoped, of course, and been determined to make something of himself...to feel capable.

He'd sought that feeling for a long time. Had only truly found it when his professional gambles had paid off. Before that it had been as if he were constantly walking on shaky ground. One wrong step and he'd go crashing down.

Echoes of that feeling had followed him the moment Gio had called, begging Elliott to go to some small island he'd never heard of and take charge of a project he had no experience with. They were louder now, after talking with Morgan, and he refused to hear them. Simply *refused* to allow himself to go back to feeling like a helpless kid.

'You said you have experience with property developers,' he said. 'How?'

She didn't seem concerned by his bluntness. 'I'm what they call a property expert. And by "they", I mean me—because that's what I call myself.'

She took a card from her back pocket and handed it to him. It was warm, and he tried not to think about the fact that it had been clinging to her butt. Her butt was of no consequence to him.

Feeling warmer than he had seconds ago, he studied the card. It had her name and contact details on it, along with her title: Property Expert.

'I appraise properties based on the owner's needs and tell them what can be done to meet those needs,' she continued.

'Would you do that for *my* needs?' he asked, and froze. That hadn't come out the way he'd meant it to. It had somehow sounded suggestive. Seductive. Neither of those were possible—he didn't even find her attractive.

Liar.

'I'm not sure what you mean,' Morgan answered slowly. 'What *are* your needs, Mr Abel?'

Arousal beat from a primal place inside him right to between his legs.

Okay, he finally admitted. Maybe he *was* attracted to her.

'Stop calling me that,' he said tersely.

'It's your name.'

'My name is Elliott.'

'Would you like me to call you Elliott?'

He nodded.

'Fine,' she agreed, unperturbed. 'What are your needs, Elliott?'

He'd thought that would be better. He'd been wrong.

Elliott, stop.

Yes, he silently answered that voice in his head.

He would not think about his needs.

He would not think about her needs.

Although he'd bet he could meet them.

He'd bet he could meet her needs for a long, long time.

Elliott.

'What do I need to do for the estate?' he questioned. 'Hypothetically. If I chose not to demolish and rebuild, what would I have to do?'

'Hmm…' It was all she said for a few minutes. Then, 'Well, I can actually answer that pretty thoroughly. I've spent a long time thinking about it.'

She pushed her hair back, straightened her shoulders. She'd shifted into professional mode. He had no idea how he knew it—or why he found her just as appealing as when she was relaxed.

'There are structural issues with a number of the houses, yes, but they don't need to be demolished—only repaired. Most of the changes I would suggest are superficial. Updating décor, making the estate look more cohesive… That last thing is what I plan to do for the wedding.' She folded her arms. 'I've consulted on estates that have needed much more work than Flipper Estate. And, now that I think about it, I'm sure the work that needs to be done here could be done in a month.'

And just like that, he came up with his own plan.

'Great. Then that's what we'll do.'

CHAPTER TWO

MORGAN'S EYES NARROWED. 'Excuse me?'

'We'll renovate the estate together. Instead of tearing down and rebuilding, we'll fix and redecorate. It'll be done by the time the wedding comes along, and you and I will both get what we want.'

There was a beat of silence before Morgan threw back her head and laughed. It exposed the column of her throat. Silky brown skin Elliott saw himself licking. The husky sound didn't do anything to rein in his desire, nor did the way the sound somehow *sparkled*.

He'd never been this distracted during a business meeting—and that was what this was, despite her personal motivations. Despite his. He was going to convince her to do this. And when he succeeded Flipper Estate would be the only place tourists wanted to stay when they came to Penguin Island.

It wasn't what his brother had asked of him. But Elliott wouldn't be able to do what Gio had asked—at least not for a month. He'd been on the island for a week, and he'd already encountered more obstacles than Gio had prepared him for. Each obstacle had made him feel increasingly helpless. But this… This idea… He could make it work, and he'd be doing it his way. He'd save his brother and his father's company time and money, and he'd get back to his own life in a month.

Back to pretending you don't have a family at all.

'You're serious?' Morgan said, laughter fading. 'You *can't* be serious.'

'What about this makes you think I'm not serious?'

'It's ludicrous, that's what.'

She began to pace across the pathway, stopping just before her feet hit the grass. Which meant she had all of a metre to do so. He wondered if she was getting dizzy from spinning so quickly.

'I'm here for the wedding. I can't take on a project this big.' She cast a look over him. 'And apparently hold your hand while I'm doing it.'

'I thought you were an expert.'

'I *am* an expert. And it's my expert opinion that this is ludicrous.'

'Morgan,' he said, as if saying her name wouldn't trip him up, 'this is the deal. You help me with the estate and your grandmother's wedding goes on as planned. We'll pay for every change that needs to be made, including what you want to do for the wedding video. Edna's getting married in the estate garden, correct?' She nodded. 'Well, we'll absorb the costs for whatever needs to be done to make the garden wedding-ready.' He'd take care of that bill himself. 'Do we have a deal?'

She stopped. Looked at him. 'You're blackmailing me?'

He offered her a benign smile. 'Only because you tried to blackmail me first.'

She pursed her lips. Put her hands on her hips. And, although he couldn't be sure, he thought she tried to hide a smile.

'Touché.' She sighed. 'But can I at least have some time to think about it? Speak with my grandmother?'

'Of course. Call me when you're ready.'

Morgan nodded, her dark brown eyes flitting over face. 'You're not what I expected, Elliott.'

With those words, she turned around and disappeared into her grandmother's house. He stared after her, then turned himself, and made his way back to the house he was staying in.

It was perched on top of a hill overlooking the beach and had the most breathtaking views. But those views were nothing in comparison to actually being on the beach.

He walked across the sand to the path that led to the house, the ocean crashing a short distance from his feet. The sun lowered at the horizon, casting a gorgeous orange glow across the sky.

There were only four or five people ahead of him, two or three behind, and that was puzzling. There should be families with children shrieking. Adults with drinks and snacks. People on dates or lazy walks. There should be laughter and happiness and an energy that made everyone grateful it was summer.

There was none of that.

It wasn't the first time he'd noticed the island was struggling. A lot of the houses around where he was staying stood empty, though they shouldn't be. Not in summer, and not with those views. Some of the beachfront commercial properties were empty, too, boarded up with 'Closed' or 'For Sale' signs.

He didn't know the history of Penguin Island, but it wouldn't surprise him if his brother and father had bought Flipper Estate *because* the island was struggling. It was exactly like them to try and save an entire island. Elliott supposed there wasn't much else they could do after everything they'd already achieved.

Still, reviving a dying island was a little over the top.

What his father and brother's intentions were wasn't his concern, though. He was only here to do what he'd been asked. And now that he'd formulated a plan to do it, he felt better about agreeing. He no longer felt as if he was floundering, driven by guilt to help the family he'd distanced himself from, and the resentment that they'd asked him at all had gone down to a simmer. He could live with a simmer.

His own business could survive without his physical presence for a month. He'd known that when he'd said yes to Gio. Their father would be back at work by then, and Gio would have hired someone to help him run things while their father had to take it easy. In the meantime, Elliott would work on this and look after his own business as often as he could. Which would be enough now that he had Morgan on his side.

She was a force of nature. Sneaky and smart. But she wouldn't push him off balance again. Yes, she'd had a tactical advantage during their first meeting, but she'd be a fool to think that would ever be repeated. She was no fool. Enticing, beautiful, sharp—but not a fool. He would do well to remember that.

And all the while to forget the attraction dangling from an invisible hook between them.

'I'm not sure about this offer,' Morgan told her grandmother. 'I had his feet to the fire, yet somehow, he ended up unscathed and *I'm* the one with the burns. Imagine how sneaky he'll be during the deal.'

Edna finished making tea and brought their mugs to the couch, where Morgan sat. Her kitchen, living room and dining area were all spread across a large open space. Apart from the kitchen island, the designations for each of the rooms were created by her grandmother's own furniture.

A four-seater table marked the dining area. It stood to the left of them, near windows that offered a glimpse of the ocean. The couches they were currently sitting on, along with the television cabinet and the coffee table, formed the living room. The kitchen was just beyond them.

All of it would have been stunning if her grandmother hadn't insisted on such drab décor.

'He won't accept your offer if you don't agree to his terms,' Edna said, her voice sharp, though her expression was strained.

Morgan reached out and squeezed her hand. 'Don't worry about it, Gran. Your wedding is going to be perfect. It'll be exactly as you imagined it.'

'Thank you, dear.' Edna patted her hand. 'But I don't want you to spread yourself too thin. You've already agreed to help with the preparations for the wedding.'

'Which includes making sure the estate is beautiful enough to appear in the video.'

'Oh, this video business is getting on my nerves.' Edna reached for her mug with a huff. 'I know Stanley's son is a famous videographer, but the pressure he's putting us under to make sure everything looks good enough to be "worthy of his name"…' She rolled her eyes. 'I don't *want* it to be worthy of his name. I just want nice memories of my day.'

It wasn't the first time Edna had complained about this. Morgan knew that, because the first time Edna had complained Morgan had offered to take on that part of the preparations. She'd been sure two weeks would be enough time to do the painting and the landscaping, so she'd told her team she'd be unavailable for that time before the wedding.

Now two weeks had turned into a month. Her business wouldn't suffer too much for it, since most of her projects at home were in the end stages, and she'd apologised to her clients, telling them she'd still be available virtually should they need her. Then she'd taken the first flight to Penguin Island to help her grandmother with the Elliott situation.

She only hoped her parents and siblings would survive her absence, too.

They're adults, Morgan, she told herself sternly. *They can handle themselves.*

Her parents had always been adults, though, and that hadn't ever been true for them.

'I'm going to do it,' she declared, making the decision.

'Morgan—'

'I'm not going to let him spoil your day!' she

exclaimed over the inner voice that asked her what the hell she was doing.

If she kept busy she wouldn't be thinking about her family at home. Her grandmother needed her more than they did and, since she couldn't physically split herself into two, she had to be here now. There was no point in worrying about them.

'Are you sure?' Edna asked, hunching her shoulders.

Whenever she did that, Morgan noticed her age. The wrinkles on her hands and around her eyes. The way time had taken her previous straight posture and curved it slightly.

Yes, she'd made the right decision. Her grandmother needed her more than her parents did. More than her siblings did. 'I'm sure.'

'Thank you, darling.'

'Of course, Gran.' Morgan smiled. 'And maybe afterwards you'll finally admit I'm your favourite grandchild.'

'Morgan.' Edna frowned. 'Every time you say that I think the others will hear.'

'It's true, though.'

'It is not.'

But Edna winked at her, making her laugh. Making her even more certain of her decision.

Now she only had to tell Elliott.

CHAPTER THREE

ELLIOTT LIFTED A hand to knock at Edna's door, but it opened before he could do so.

'Elliott,' Edna said with a nod when she saw him standing there.

'Good morning,' he replied in the same tone.

They had only been polite in the last week, though an edge had lined every conversation Edna had had with him. It didn't seem to be there any more. Did that mean Morgan was going to accept his offer or deny it?

'Morgan asked me to come.'

Edna nodded again. 'She's inside. Good luck.'

He watched her go past him, wondering about her words. Her shoulders were straight, her feet bare, even though the rest of her was dressed warmly. There had been a chill in the air that day. The ocean was making it worse, with mist and fog hovering over its surface, spreading its fingers out towards them.

'It's too cold to walk barefoot,' Elliott muttered.

'Yes.'

A voice came from behind him. He turned to find Morgan standing in the doorway, her eyes on her grandmother's retreating figure.

'But she goes for walks in the rain like that, too. It's part of her ritual, no matter the weather.'

'No shoes?' Elliott asked, looking for Edna. The fog had swallowed her up entirely now. 'She's asking to catch a cold.'

'Hmm…'

He turned back. Narrowed his eyes.

'It's nothing,' she said, then seemed to change her mind. 'You almost sound concerned.'

'What if I am?'

'It would be unusual.'

'Why?'

Morgan shoved her hands into her jersey's pockets. It was long, pockets aligned with her thighs, so the movement didn't quite seem right. But it was enough to get him to look at her.

Two days ago, when he'd first seen her, he'd been too surprised to spare more than a casual thought for how she looked. Then, she'd worn black trousers and a sleeveless black top. Functional and appropriate—which, now that he thought about it, was probably what she'd intended. But today she was casual.

It broke his brain.

How could her tights cling so wonderfully to her legs? Long, *full* legs that gave him visions of them wrapped around his waist. Her jersey was much bigger than her right size, yet it did nothing to hide the lush curves of her body, especially when she put her hands in her pockets, dragging the material down, tight over her chest. It highlighted her breasts, which were…bigger than he remembered.

Did she mean to torture him?

'You haven't seemed that concerned about my grandmother's well-being before,' she said in that husky voice of hers.

He blinked. He wasn't there to ogle her; this was business. Not to mention that she was right. He *hadn't* been all that concerned about her grandmother. A wave of guilt crashed at the shore of his consciousness and he shifted uncomfortably.

But there was nothing he could do about it now.

'Can I come inside?'

Morgan studied him, then nodded and gestured for him to enter. As she closed the door, Elliott took a look at the place. He'd seen the basic design in the blueprints Gio had forwarded him, had even seen a few of the empty houses when he'd done his inspection days ago, but he'd never been inside an occupied one.

It had life. When someone lived in one of these houses it had life. Although the décor in this one was an odd choice. The indigo walls were too dark, the furniture and carpets too heavy. But the cups on the coffee table to one side; the plants on every spare surface of the house; the photo frames and paintings on the walls; the throws on the couches; the dishes in the kitchen cabinets— that was all life, all living, and it made him see what was so appealing about developing spaces that would result in other houses like this.

'Coffee?' she asked.

'Please.'

He contemplated the couch, but went to the kitchen instead. It felt wrong to sit down while she was working.

Strange. He'd never thought something like that before.

He cleared his throat. 'Can I help?'

'Not with the coffee,' she answered, her back to him.

His eyes skimmed over her. The jersey covered her butt, but left most of her thighs on view. His first impression of them had been correct: they were magnificent. He thought about how they'd feel in his hands, around his waist...

'Elliott?' Morgan looked over her shoulder. Her hair was pulled away from her face today, with a ribbon of some kind that made the waves of it flutter down her back. 'Did you hear a word I said?'

'Yes, of course.' He paused, searching his mind for anything she might have said. When he came up with nothing, he cleared his throat again. 'You want me not to help with the coffee.'

'And then I pointed to those biscuits over there and asked if you could plate them.' She turned with two mugs, placing them on the kitchen island. 'But clearly that request must have short-circuited your brain.'

It wasn't the request.

To distract himself, he moved to where she pointed, finding a glass container with what looked like chocolate chip cookies inside.

'Plate?' he asked.

'The cupboard above you.'

There was something that sounded amused in her voice, but he didn't look at her. Wouldn't give her the satisfaction of seeing that he was distracted, or any idea that his distraction was because of her. She was turning him into someone he didn't recognise—or perhaps someone he recognised too well. Someone he'd worked hard to leave behind.

He gritted his teeth, put the biscuits on a plate and added the plate to the island with the coffees. She had cream and sugar waiting for him.

'Black,' he said, with a quick shake of his head.

She nodded and pushed one of the cups towards him. Relief flooded his body. She hadn't handed it to him. Which meant he wouldn't look like an idiot, trying to avoid touching her fingers. And he would have had to. His awareness of her was too dangerous…too insidious to risk a careless touch.

When he met her gaze she was watching him, her eyebrows high, her brown eyes wide open. Had he noticed how rich they were before? How they looked like a thousand-year-old bottle of brown liquor, the finest there was, something owned by an emperor or a queen or someone equally important? When they were open like that he imagined falling into them, into the depths of them, and drowning. Getting drunk on her.

His skin prickled.

He clenched his jaw again, resisting a harsh exhalation.

'I take it you've come to a decision?' he asked. His words had been snippier than he'd intended. He could tell by the way she straightened, though her gaze was still curious.

'I'll do it.'

The relief that came now was more powerful than that he'd felt before. And it was joined by a faint buzz of excitement...of anticipation.

'I'm pleased.'

'I thought you might be.'

'Why?'

'Because you're getting exactly what you want,' she answered, her expression puzzled. 'And you're getting it from me.'

It took him a second to focus on the less dirty implication of her words. 'It seems you're good at your job.'

'Thank you.'

She said it the same way he imagined she'd say, *I know.*

'You're not upset that I looked you up?'

Her puzzlement deepened. 'Why would I be? I looked you up, too. It's only fair that you do the same with me. Although I probably won't like how deep a dive you've probably done.'

'Skeletons in your closet?'

She snorted. 'I'm an open book.'

Was that why he kept asking her questions? Was he trying to figure out how her brain worked? Could he sense that she'd answer all his questions? Simply tell him everything he wanted to know?

It was all to get ahead of her, he told himself.

Even though he knew he was lying.

'Now that you're willing to help,' he said briskly, 'I assume we won't be encountering any "obstacles"?' She shook her head. 'In that case, I'd like to ask you something.'

'What?' she asked suspiciously.

'Has the island always been this quiet?'

Her eyes flickered. 'No. Penguin Island used to be…' She shook her head. 'Busy. Bustling. People used to go to the penguin sanctuary. The beaches used to be packed. There were many more restaurants on the beach than there currently are, and people couldn't get a seat without a reservation.'

He'd done his research and had found a story in the papers detailing as much. It had been on page eight of the paper, which in itself had told him that people no longer cared about the island as much as they used to.

It was a sad situation, since Cape Town had once been considered Penguin Island's mainland and Capetonians had made their way to the island whenever they could. But somehow things had tapered off. The penguin sanctuary had started losing its funding. More and more of the animals had been moved to a sanctuary in Cape Town. Soon, only long-time visitors had spent their summers on the island. People had begun losing their jobs, and because of it Penguin Island was now losing its residents.

'It's still an amazing island,' Morgan continued fiercely. 'It has everything Cape Town has to offer, but with more peace. The people here deserve better.'

She sounded deflated. An impulse rose up, nearly spilled out of his mouth. He clamped his teeth. Took a moment to regroup.

He wasn't about to make this offer because of *her*. Because she was sad that the island where her grandmother lived—where people loved her—was struggling. He was doing it because it made financial and logical sense.

Calibrated now, he nodded. 'Do you think there are enough people available here to work on the estate revamp with you?'

* * *

Morgan stared.

And then, when she was done staring, she stared some more.

'You want to hire people from the island to work on the revamp?'

'If there are enough people available.' He dipped his head. 'Are there?'

She thought about all the places that had closed in the last couple of years. The ice-cream parlour down the road from Flipper Estate. The café a short walk across the beach. The two beachfront restaurants that had closed within months of each other.

Every time something like that happened her grandmother would call to tell her. Not because of the loss of business, but because of her friends who had lost their jobs. What Elliott was proposing would be huge for those people. She couldn't quite believe it.

'Why don't you believe it?' Elliott said, sounding affronted.

Oops. Had she said that last part out loud?

'I do.'

'Sounds like it.'

She snorted softly at his dry tone, then pushed her coffee aside, squared her shoulders. 'There are enough people available. But most of them won't have any experience.'

He leaned back against the kitchen island,

folded his arms. Her eyes flickered to his biceps. She couldn't figure out her fascination with them. They were big, and obviously muscular, but not so defined that they looked artificial. She didn't understand that description. Nor did she understand her compulsion to reach out, run a finger over the veins she saw there…cover both arms with her hands and squeeze.

She reached for her coffee, taking a huge gulp and biting back her wince at the heat.

'We'll leave the work requiring specialised knowledge to experts. But I'm assuming a lot of it is mainly manual labour, which most people can do.'

He looked expectantly at her.

'That's true,' she said.

She reached for a biscuit, sank her teeth into it.

'And you'll be there to supervise.'

'Me?' she answered after she'd swallowed. 'What do you mean?'

'You said you'd take the lead with the renovations.'

'No, I said I'd *help* with them. As in, help you figure out what needs to be done where. Maybe draw up some plans for the interior design.' She took another bite. Chewed. Swallowed. 'I did not say I'd take the lead on a project I know next to nothing about, stepping on the toes of the professionals you've hired and taking up my time.'

An eyebrow lifted. Her stomach did a cartwheel. She bit into another piece of biscuit, because his sexiness was stressing her out. Not to mention what he was asking of her, which was much more than she'd thought she was agreeing to, and exactly what she'd been worried about when she'd told her grandmother about it.

But he was offering work to people she cared about. People who needed the money.

'I guess we didn't understand one another,' he said.

She took a breath. 'No.' She finished her biscuit and took another. 'But I'll do it.'

'Are you sure?' he asked mildly. 'Because there are only three biscuits left.'

She stopped chewing. 'What are you saying?'

'You've seemed a little…obsessed.'

'I'm stress eating. But I can stress eat and negotiate at the same time.'

The side of his mouth lifted and, man, oh, man, did it do amazing things to his beautiful face. It was a terrible time to focus on it when she had only the day before noticed it somewhat disinterestedly. But now her brain was all *Look at his brooding eyebrows! His full lips! Those cheekbones! His perfectly crooked nose!*

If she'd been interested in dating at all, she probably would have been interested in dating him. But relationships weren't for people who were always holding their families together. She'd learnt that the hard way, a long time ago. A relationship had distracted her, and she hadn't been there when her sister had needed her. Their parents had had to step in, and the anxiety that had caused for both her and Hattie had been...

Well, Morgan hadn't cared for it. Since then, she'd made sure no one would experience it again. At least not because of her choices.

Which was why deciding to help her grandmother had been tough. But her grandmother was family, too, and Morgan had made sure her siblings knew she was still reachable by phone. Hopefully there wouldn't be an emergency that required her presence. If there was, Penguin Island was a two-hour flight away...

She exhaled. Briefly considered stuffing the rest of the biscuit into her mouth. The only thing that stopped her was the way Elliott was staring at her.

Oh, yes. Elliott was still there.

At least she wasn't thinking about his beautifully crooked nose any more.

'I didn't mean to stress you out,' Elliott said. 'Nor did I think we were negotiating.'

'Of course we are.' She set the half-eaten biscuit down. 'You'll have to talk to your team. Make sure they're okay with me taking the lead. Arrange for a meeting so that I can speak with them, too.'

'You wouldn't trust what I tell you?'

'I don't think so, no,' she answered honestly.

'Somehow, in every conversation we've had, you've come out ahead. You're someone who manages to do whatever it takes to *be* ahead. And you're so skilled at doing it that the person you're doing it to doesn't realise what's happened until it's too late.'

His mouth twitched, but he only said, 'This coming from the person who tricked me into meeting with her, then ambushed me?'

'It was hardly an ambush.'

'You're not really the right person to make that call, are you?'

They stared at one another. It wasn't quite a challenge, but it might as well have been. Each second increased the tension. And the increased tension made her heart beat faster. Her skin grow clammier. She felt as if she were in a sauna and someone was incrementally turning up the heat. She'd collapse soon if she wasn't careful.

She was nothing if not careful.

'I'm good at what I do, Elliott. But I can't be good if the team I'm working with doesn't trust me. *That's* why I want to meet with them. If they trust me, they'll trust that I'll be able to manage the untrained people we're bringing in, and the project will go a lot smoother.' She paused. 'If we do this right, Flipper Estate could draw in tourists. Tourists with money they can spend on the island.'

She didn't continue because she didn't have

to. He would know that if people started staying at the estate, spending their money on the island, the economy would be reinvigorated. If that happened, the island could invest in its tourism industry again. The sanctuary could reopen. The activities that had died off would come back, more people would want to vacation here, and Flipper Estate would pay for itself in half the time she imagined Elliott's family had banked on.

And, yes, all of that would mean higher employment rates for the people who'd lost their jobs.

She had to consider that Elliott had thought about this, too, since he was hiring some of those people for this job. She'd judged him as shrewd and uncaring, but perhaps she wasn't being fair—though the green and gold storm of emotion in his eyes tried to convince her otherwise. Maybe he was shrewd, but not totally uncaring. Either way, she found herself holding her breath until he spoke.

'I'd like the names of everyone you'll want to put forward for the work. We'll need the admin sorted as soon as possible—though we might have to start before everything is finalised.'

'That won't be a problem.'

'I can arrange for a meeting at the end of the week. I still have employees trickling in.'

'Sure.' She bit her lip. 'Thank you.'

He nodded. 'I take it our negotiation is complete?'

'My grandmother's wedding remains a priority.'

'I have no doubt about that,' he answered dryly. 'If you need anything to achieve that, even if it doesn't actually pertain to the project, you know where to find me.'

Not totally uncaring, indeed.

Pleasure bloomed inside her, but she stamped it down.

No pleasure. Only business.

'Thank you,' she said firmly.

'We have a deal.'

He pushed himself off the counter and offered her his hand. After a beat, she took it. His hand was much larger than hers, rougher, too, as if he personally made the furniture his company 'Crafted' sold. It sent a shiver down her spine, but she told herself it wasn't erotic. It was concern.

She was worried that she'd just made the biggest mistake of her life.

CHAPTER FOUR

WHEN ELLIOTT HAD first arrived on Penguin Island he'd thought it quaint. The main road—creatively called Beach Road, since it ended at the beach that made the island's perimeter—formed a cross that divided the island into four. Two of the quadrants were mainly residential areas, where the houses ranged from the most beautiful beach homes to more dilapidated ones, worn by the salt of the ocean. The third quadrant was reserved for the now-closed penguin sanctuary, which was the wildest beach of the island. He was currently in the fourth quadrant, that held the harbour and the main town.

Somehow, quaintness had turned into wonder.

It was the kind of place that didn't entirely feel like part of South Africa. The cobblestones were more suited to an English town, as were the narrow paths between the stores, with more people walking than using cars. But the colourful storefronts were one hundred percent South African, as was the energy. It held a friendliness, a welcomeness that he'd never experienced before in the travelling he'd done in his life. He could smell the ocean from here, too, and if he kept perfectly still he could hear the faint wash of the waves against the shore.

The paths weren't busy this morning, despite the fact that they held the heart of the town. The grocery stores, the pharmacies, the doctors' offices and the dentist.

The closer he got to the harbour, the more touristy the places became. A coffee shop, a restaurant and a gift shop, all with penguin-themed décor—and, in the case of the gift shop, merchandise. And there were enough empty buildings that it felt almost ominous.

An uncomfortable feeling settled in his chest. He tried to identify its source. It took time, but eventually he realised it came from the conversation he'd had with Morgan. She'd made him feel almost responsible for reviving the town by telling him the renovation of Flipper Estate could be more than simply that. That it could draw tourists into the town. She'd all but said that it could lead to an improved economy, and there had been hope in her eyes as she'd envisaged a future where the islanders had work again...

Yeah, that had made him uncomfortable.

He didn't want to be responsible for an economy. Hell, he didn't even want to be responsible for the renovation, and he was doing that for his *family*.

Although, to be fair, he hadn't wanted to do anything for his family in a long time. He was content with being the outsider. The son who only visited his parents on special occasions. Doing more than that tended to make him feel small. Reminded him of the kid he used to be, who wanted nothing more than his parents' unconditional love and approval.

He wasn't a kid any more, and he knew he'd never get either of those things. Stepping in for the Penguin Island project was a favour to his brother, who he had a decent relationship with. A cordial one, at least. And, fine, he was also doing it because his father couldn't work immediately after his heart attack.

But helping out didn't mean he was that kid again. Helping out was the kind of thing even a 'special occasions only' son did. Plus, Elliott was helping on his own terms. He hadn't told his brother about those terms yet—about any of the changes he was planning, really—but Gio had other, more important things on his mind. He wasn't worried about one project when he had several others he was handling by himself.

'Elliott. *Elliott.*' A peppy voice sounded from behind him. 'Why aren't you moving?'

He turned, looking for the voice and finding it lower down than he expected. He adjusted his gaze to see big brown eyes blinking up at him. Morgan. Her long, wavy hair drifted to her face from her ponytail and she pushed it back, irritated.

Charming.

What? No. It wasn't charming. Why would he find it charming? That irritation? That tiny movement? Why would realising she was shorter than he remembered be charming, too? Why would it make his body ache?

It wouldn't.

Good thing he didn't find *her* charming either.

'Distracted,' he said in a short tone.

Seemed he always spoke to her in a short tone. What was wrong with him?

'Hmm…' Even that sounded peppy. 'Shall we go inside?'

He gestured for her to lead the way.

Everyone working at the coffee shop they were meeting at greeted her by name, asked about her family, and only then acknowledged his presence. Because of it, he learnt that she was the oldest of three siblings, that she doted on her niece, and that her entire family would be in town for the wedding, just over three weeks away.

'I'm sorry about that,' she said when they were finally seated. 'I haven't been around for a while.'

'Why not?'

She blinked. 'Oh. I… I've been busy.'

The way her eyelashes fluttered, the way she

frowned, told him that wasn't the truth. Or maybe it was, but it wasn't the whole truth. He shouldn't want to know what the whole truth was. He *didn't* want to know.

'Maybe if I hadn't been so busy I'd have seen what was happening here,' she continued, so softly he would have thought she wasn't speaking to him if it hadn't been for her next words. 'My grandmother told me about places closing, people moving away... I don't know why I didn't put it together.'

'You were in denial.'

She met his gaze. 'Is that meant to make me feel better?'

'Yes.'

She smiled then, highlighting the bright red she'd painted her lips with. She'd done some other things to her face, too. Her eyes were sharper, which was probably why he'd noticed them earlier. There was something different about her cheeks as well. He knew make-up was responsible for all of it, but he couldn't figure out what exactly she'd done.

'You have an odd way of comforting people, Elliott.'

'I wasn't—'

He broke off. No point in denying it. He had been trying to comfort her. His cheeks grew warm, but he knew it couldn't be a blush. A blush would mean he was embarrassed. Self-conscious. He was neither.

'I've had an idea,' she said briskly, as if she were aware of his inner turmoil and wanted to move on. 'To boost the estate's profile once we're done.'

He nodded. 'Go on.'

'My grandmother's soon-to-be son-in-law is a well-known wedding videographer. He has a huge social media following, and has shot a few celebrity weddings, some politicians, a couple of millionaires...' She picked up a sugar sachet and began to fiddle with it. 'He's doing his father and my grandmother's wedding, too—hence their demands for how the estate should look.'

'You're doing it for *him*?'

She gave him a look. 'My grandmother doesn't care about how the houses in the estate look. She loves living there. It's home to her. Although she *is* getting married in the garden, which is objectively stunning, so maybe she does care?' She tilted her head. 'But I don't think she would have asked me to redo the facades of the houses if there hadn't been some pressure from Gerald to make sure the venue was "worthy of his amazing name".'

She rolled her eyes and took a second sugar sachet, hitting it against the first. Was she pretending it was Gerald's head? Maybe she was pretending it was Elliott's. After all, he'd been as much of a pain in the neck as this Gerald.

Again, he told himself that he didn't care. But his mind refused the lie this time. He *did* care. He cared that he'd been short with her, and that she seemed to think he was so cold and unfeeling that he wouldn't care about her grandmother's health—that her perception of him was that he'd do anything to get ahead.

It made no sense when he'd actually cultivated that image. Not only with her, but with the world. When he'd left the needy child he'd once been behind. The child who'd been desperate for his parents' attention. Who'd wanted to be treated as well as his genius brother. He'd purposely put a barrier between his emotions and everyone else's, in business and his personal life, and it had suited him perfectly fine. Hell, it had turned him into a success.

But you have no real relationships because of it.

'That was a little bit of a rant, wasn't it?' she asked, biting her lip.

He focused on her again, his gaze lingering on her lips. He'd been distracted, had made her feel uncomfortable because he hadn't been paying attention, and now he was staring at her. Because a particular part of his body had taken note of her lip-biting.

He shook his head. 'It's fine.' He took a breath. 'Your idea…?'

'Right.' She put down the sugar. 'What if we get him to post the wedding on his social media? We can ask everyone on the island to share it, using a hashtag like *romanceisland*, and get Penguin Island trending?'

'Get everyone's attention?'

'The right people, too,' she agreed. 'The kind of people who would hire a wedding videographer like Gerald. If he can get footage of the beaches, the forests, the town… This place is beautiful, Elliott. There's no way people won't be tempted into getting married here. And with his shots of Flipper Estate they'll know there are gorgeous modern homes to rent for their guests. The garden is beautiful. We can build an altar, or a floral arch—something to signal that *this* is where they want to declare they'll be spending their lives with the person they love.' She leaned forward, pressing her hands into the table. 'It could be amazing.'

He stared. Because her idea was good. Great, really. It would do everything that she said, and quickly, too. People with money wanted the exclusivity of being the first to do something. He knew, because he'd fallen into that trap more than once and was vaguely ashamed of it. If she was right, people would be trying to secure the island for their weddings quickly. She'd probably considered that, too.

It *was* a great idea.

But mostly he stared because of her. Because she was beautiful when she was passionate. It kicked him in the gut, and he had to cling to his breath so the air didn't escape his lungs.

'You hate it,' she said, slumping over.

'No.' He cleared his throat when the word came out hoarse. 'No, it's good. Brilliant.'

'Brilliant? Really?' She picked up the sugar sachet again. 'Someone should tell your face.'

'My face?'

'You look like someone just informed you of a close friend's passing.'

Considering he felt as if he was grieving— for his sanity and for the version of himself who didn't get distracted by attraction—that made sense.

'That's not a reflection of my feelings on this issue.' *Only about you.* 'Your idea really is good. But it means we *have* to be done by the wedding.'

'I know.'

'That's just over three weeks.'

'I know that, too.' The sugar sachets returned to their rightful place. 'You said the meeting with your team is tomorrow?' He nodded. 'Once we have them on board, we'll need to meet with the people we're hiring for the construction work. We'll need a bigger venue, so we should probably use the Town Hall. The big building on the hill,' she clarified, nodding her head in its general direction.

'Won't booking that take time?'

'This is Penguin Island,' she said with faint amusement. 'If the mayor approves, we'll have it. For tomorrow night, too.'

'Of course we will.'

She smiled. 'The joys of a small town.'

'What do we tell them?' he asked, ignoring the slight racing of his heart.

'What we've been saying all along. It'll be hard work in a short time frame. We'll explain exactly what needs to be done and how we intend on doing it. If you can get the paperwork ready by tomorrow, we can have everyone sign it.'

'I can do that.'

'Good.' She sat back. 'We'll be ready to start the day after tomorrow, and then it'll be full steam ahead.'

'You're good at this,' he said, without thinking.

The words were true, but if he'd given himself a chance to consider them he would have tried… Well, not to say them. It felt revealing. He wasn't sure how or why.

But then her expression softened. Grew vulnerable. There were a thousand secrets in her brown eyes when she met his gaze, and when she smiled, it seemed sad.

'Thank you.' Even her voice sounded raw. 'I've had a lot of practice at fixing things.'

And that practice had hurt her.

He had no idea how he knew that, but he did, and he was getting ready to avenge her when she shook her head.

'We should talk to Mayor Henderson about the Town Hall.'

All business now, he saw. 'Tell me how it goes.'

'Oh, no,' she said with a snort. 'When I said "we", I meant you.'

'He doesn't know me.'

She wrinkled her nose. 'That's probably for the best.'

CHAPTER FIVE

THERE WAS A reason Morgan didn't date any more—and that reason began with the mayor of Penguin Island. He hadn't been mayor back then, of course. Back then he'd been a confident, cool, charming boy who'd given Morgan her first kiss. Been her *almost* first lover.

She'd lost her judgement, just like many other people did when they were young and naïve.

Most of those people didn't have parents to look after, though. Two younger siblings to take care of.

'You have history with Mayor Henderson,' Elliott stated.

It *had* been a statement, but it was as if his voice hadn't told his face. His eyebrows were raised, not for the first time during their conversation. In disbelief? Surprise? Judgement?

She didn't care.

Don't you?

No, I don't, she told her traitorous inner voice.

'We had a thing once upon a time.'

The brows lifted higher. 'You and Mayor Henderson?'

'He was just Thaddeus Jerome Henderson the Third when we dated.' She snorted at the look on his face. 'Yeah, I generally feel that way when I think about that part of my life. So I try not to.'

Elliott didn't reply, but he looked at her. Really looked at her. As if he could see into her soul. As if he could draw out her secrets, have them reveal themselves to him, and then he'd have some magical power over her.

It felt as if he was using a measure of that power now. The way his eyes searched her face, met her gaze, lingered. She held her breath, clung to her secrets, and knew it was silly.

Pointless, too, apparently, because he said, 'He hurt you?'

'No.'

Quick, simple denial. She should have left it at that. She didn't.

'I hurt him.'

'I have no doubt about that.'

'What does that mean?'

'Nothing.'

His denial came as quickly as hers had, but it didn't feel simple. Not in the least.

'Look, we dated one summer when I was in my early twenties.'

Why was she explaining this to him? Why couldn't she *stop*?

'Half of the time we spent here, the other half back home in Cape Town, and it was…' She exhaled. 'Exactly what you'd expect from a relationship when you're young and stupid.'

For a while, 'young and stupid' had been glorious. Morgan had been a young adult, but Thad had been her first boyfriend. Her first relationship. He hadn't been the first person interested in her, but before that she'd been too consumed by her family responsibilities. Too haunted by the ghosts of the past.

When her parents had had Morgan, they'd been only sixteen and seventeen. Morgan had always refused to repeat their actions, so she'd stayed away from dating, from flirting, from anything that could potentially lead her down her parents' path.

It had been easy, since she'd had her siblings to look after. They were five and eight years younger than her, and the adjustment to having a bigger family had been hard for her parents. So Morgan had learned how to help. She was the older sister; of course she would help take care of them.

The year Morgan had dated Thad, her sister Hattie had ended up pregnant at seventeen, just like their mother. Her brother Rob had had his sullen teenage feelings amplified by a learning disability diagnosis. And Morgan…

Morgan had been tired.

Too tired to maintain the defences she'd tried to put in place to prevent a relationship with Thad in the first place.

It had only been Morgan who'd come to the island that summer. Hattie had been too far along in her pregnancy, and Rob had had a series of assessments he still had to work through. She hadn't wanted to come, but her grandmother had insisted. Edna had called her parents, said heaven knew what to them, and they'd insisted, too.

Morgan had agreed because of the tiredness. Because everyone had been okay with her cutting the usual time she spent visiting her grandmother in half as a compromise. Because her parents had seemed relatively calm about everything they were being left with.

And then she'd come, and Thad had charmed her, and she'd been young and stupid—hiding the relationship from her grandmother, as if Edna would have cared that her twenty-two-year-old granddaughter had a boyfriend. Rendezvousing with him in secret to keep anyone from seeing them.

When she'd returned to Cape Town, Thad had followed, and she'd lost track of herself. Sweet, innocent kisses had become passionate, desperate touches. Touches had led to caresses. To things Morgan had never imagined herself doing.

But she'd stopped them before she could make the kind of mistake she'd avoided her entire life.

And that same night Hattie had gone into labour. Something Morgan had only discovered *after* her niece's birth, since she'd turned her phone off.

Her stomach churned.

This was exactly why she didn't like thinking about it.

'Any tips?' Elliott asked now, his voice gruff, short.

It tended to be at times. She couldn't be sure, but she thought it had something to do with his control. When he felt as if he didn't have it, or when he was clinging to it.

But that didn't make sense in this context. The last few minutes had been about *her*. What did he have to control in that?

Maybe she'd thought wrong.

'Compliment him,' she said softly. 'He likes being flattered.'

'You don't seem the type to indulge a man's ego.'

'Because I haven't done it with you?' She laughed lightly, aware of the tension growing in the air. 'You're not the type of man who wants me to indulge his ego.'

A single eyebrow lifted. She felt as if she'd been dropped into a pool of hot water.

'That's confident,' he noted.

'Yes.' Needing something to do, she gestured for the bill. 'Since you're not here because Abel and Son Development is your company, I assume you're doing all this for your family. Yet you haven't really commented on me doing this for *my* family, which I've been open about. Usually, people try to find some kind of common personal ground, even in business. The fact that you haven't means you prefer to keep people at a distance, which doesn't exactly play into the whole ego thing. So, yeah,' she ended, 'I am confident.'

He didn't reply. Her heart began to pound, but she urged it to remain calm. She meant every word. Didn't regret saying it either. So the intensity in his eyes, the way he clenched and unclenched his hands, shouldn't bother her.

Then he exhaled.

'Morgan, I don't know—' He cut himself off and shook his head. 'You're—' He didn't finish that either.

'Don't hurt yourself, Elliott,' she said, amused. 'I promise to keep the mind-reading part of myself to a minimum. Now, I have some things to do before our meeting with everyone,' she went on, shifting the conversation to a subject he'd be more comfortable with. 'Assuming you can get Mayor Henderson's approval.'

'I'll get it,' he said easily, though still gruffly.

Easy, she warned her body when it shimmied at the sound of his voice. With the power of knowing she'd done it to him. *You don't even know that it's because of you.*

But, even as she told herself that, she knew it was.

She had some power over him.

And, heaven help her, she wanted to discover the extent of it.

Mayor Thaddeus Jerome Henderson the Third was an idiot.

Not within his position. The mayor—who had insisted that Elliott call him Thad—had been professional, courteous, even helpful. Elliott had managed to secure the Town Hall for their meeting, and Mayor 'Call-Me-Thad' had asked if he could be there.

'You're doing a great thing for this community,' Thad had said, threading his fingers together and laying his hands on his desk. 'If I can offer my support in any way, you'll have it.'

Of course Elliott didn't want Thad's support. He and Morgan were managing things just fine. But that thought had been tainted with personal feelings…emotions he didn't care to examine. So he'd turned that part of himself off and looked at the situation objectively.

Thad's support might not mean anything to Elliott, but the islanders who had been without jobs—who might have blamed the mayor for not doing anything about the employment situation— would be grateful. Politically, Thad would be subtly implying that he was responsible for finding them work.

Smart of him. Elliott could admit that. He wasn't

upset about it—he would have done the same thing in Thad's position. But that smartness was clearly isolated to his professional choices. In his personal life Thad had ruined a relationship with Morgan. He'd hurt her—and that made Thad an idiot.

And, yes, Morgan had said she'd hurt Thad, too, but break-ups were like that. Not that Elliott would know. He made sure all the people he dated knew what to expect up front: no attachments, no emotional connections. They got to enjoy each other's company, and that was it. Most of the time it worked. So these…these *feelings* Morgan awoke in him were as unwelcome as they were strange.

The jealousy that had him now calling a perfectly reasonable man an idiot was a good example of that.

That had started the moment she'd told him what had happened between her and Thad. He'd tried with all his might not to let the way her words had affected him show, but he didn't think he'd succeeded.

As a man who prided himself on his control, he didn't appreciate that. But his control was intact once again. So when Morgan had called to ask if they could walk to the Town Hall together, he'd agreed.

Spending time with her was an unavoidable aspect of their working relationship. He had to get used to *that*, and not his inappropriate feelings for her.

'Hey,' she said now, bounding down the path of Edna's house, her dress flying behind her. 'Thanks for walking with me.'

He nodded.

'I thought it would be good for us to arrive together. Show a united front or something?' She shrugged as they started walking towards the beach that would take them to Beach Road. 'That might be silly. But I figured since I wanted to run some of the décor choices by you, we'd use this walk productively either way.'

She continued telling him about the colour scheme she was thinking of. Suggesting that she use one of the houses as a real-life mock-up, so he could see everything. And she talked about getting her grandmother's friends to start moving out, and her grandmother, too.

Edna had always planned to move out—back to Cape Town with her fiancé, who was currently there, finalising everything for their move.

'But of course she's giving me a hard time, because she's worried you'll go back on your word.' She gave Elliott a look. 'I told her we could trust you, but I don't think she bought it. I should probably do something about that…but she'll get the chance to see you're serious. We'll have done plenty of work before we get to her house. There's time.'

He studied her as they walked down the tarred

road that led to the beach. There were houses on either side, some in disrepair, others well-kept, with tidy gardens and swing sets.

'You're nervous,' he noted. 'Why?'

'Nervous? I'm not nervous.' She bent and picked a flower from someone's garden. Twirled it a few times between her fingers before popping it behind her ear. 'What makes you think I'm nervous?'

'You haven't stopped talking since we left your grandmother's house.'

'That's not true.' Her eyes went wide. 'It *is* true. I'm sorry.'

'No, it's okay. It's…cute.'

He felt her go still rather than saw it, and his cheeks grew hot. Where had that admission come from? Yes, he'd *thought* it. Had been entertained by her constant stream of chatter. By the fact that she'd revealed a quirk. He was impressed that despite all their talks, their negotiations, she hadn't revealed the quirk earlier. Maybe she hadn't been nervous then. But she *had* been stressed, he thought, remembering the biscuit-eating. Another little charming quirk.

Cute? Charming? He needed to get a grip, and fast.

'Sorry,' he muttered. 'That was—'

'Nice,' she interrupted. 'It's nice to hear what's going on in your head. Sometimes I feel like I'm…'

'Like you're what?' he asked when she didn't finish.

'I'd rather not say.'

'I'd rather you did.'

She sighed. 'Sometimes it feels like I'm talking to a robot. You barely give me any reaction, and when you do it's…controlled. Or muted. Like you're keeping yourself from feeling, or something.'

He almost stumbled. Only pure determination kept his feet moving. One foot in front of the other. Left, right, left, right. He found himself mentally saying those words, repeating the instructions over and over again as he walked, as his feet sank into soft sand and he dropped down to take off his shoes.

How had she known that? She'd spent less than a week with him, but she'd already seen through to the core of him. There were people in his life who'd known him for longer and hadn't seen it. Or if they had, they hadn't said anything. Not even his brother, who'd known him before…

Before he'd made the decision to stop allowing his emotions to get the better of him.

'I didn't want to say it,' she said when he straightened. Her shoes were already in her hands, and she was watching him worriedly. 'I didn't want to upset you.'

'You haven't upset me.'

'You seem upset.'

'Impossible. I'm a robot.'

'No, I didn't mean—' She exhaled. 'You're reacting now,' she said. 'It's muted, but I can see that you're upset. And I'm sorry.'

There was a thickness in his throat. An irrational anger coursing through his body. Because he *was* upset, and he didn't want her to see it. And he hated that his emotions had affected her. He hated that her precise and sharp observations had made him feel raw and naked.

'You see too much,' he said eventually, walking again. 'You talk too much, too.'

She gave a light snort. 'I'm sorry for the first thing, though it makes no sense for me to apologise. It feels right, though, so that's what I'm doing. And, yes, to the second thing.' Seemingly deciding he needed a change in topic, she continued. 'I hid it from you earlier today. I knew it would scare you off.'

He almost laughed.

The desire to do so surprised him into not laughing. The confusion kept him from doing more than shaking his head. The effect this woman had on him was…impossible. Almost a decade of predictability when it came to his emotions, and now he was on a rollercoaster in a matter of minutes.

'I am nervous,' she said, changing the topic again.

For him, he thought. *Again*.

'This is important, right? It's important for your team to respect me, to think I'm capable, to be willing to work with the islanders. And it's important for the islanders to see me as more than just Edna's granddaughter—the little girl with pigtails who used to walk on the beach with her two younger siblings. Never laughing, always serious.'

'I don't believe that.'

'What?'

'The never laughing part.'

As if proving his point, she laughed again. At the same moment the wind rustled through the curls she'd pulled behind a colourful headband. Whipped through the skirt of her white summer dress. He caught a glimpse of beautiful brown thighs. Thick and luscious. Not for the first time he pictured them wrapped around his waist. It was becoming an obsession.

'I was a serious child,' she said with a shake of her head, drawing him out of his own thoughts. 'My parents…' She trailed off. 'There was a lot to think about when I was younger.'

He looked at her face, saw the struggle there. Wanted to ask. But that was hardly fair. He refused to say anything personal to her. And even though he knew she was dying to ask, she never did. She respected his boundaries, so he would respect hers.

So heaven only knew why he blurted out, 'My brother is a genius.'

He stopped walking. So did she. She was watching him now, her face filled with puzzlement.

Of course it was. He'd just blurted out an inane piece of information with no context. A personal piece of information, something he never spoke of. *Never.*

'A genius?' she repeated. 'Is that something your mother told you? Because it's sweet, but not worthy of that kind of proclamation.'

His lips curved, his amusement faint but there. He looked down, trying to figure out how to explain. He couldn't not explain. Not when he'd brought it up in the first place.

'No, he's an actual genius. He went for IQ tests. Evaluations. Ended up going to university at fifteen, finishing at eighteen, and then helping my father run his business.'

Increasing production and turnover by two hundred per cent in five years.

He didn't add that part, though it was etched in his brain. When his father had started what had then been Abel Property Development, the company had been moderately successful. Then Gio had begun to implement his plans, and moderate success had turned into significant success.

His parents had framed every newspaper article. There had already been walls in their house dedicated to Gio. To his awards, his degrees. The newspaper stories had joined them. And by the time Elliott had turned eighteen, ready to go to university himself, with good grades, he'd already felt like a failure.

'Elliott...' Morgan breathed as she came closer. 'I'm sorry for the pain that caused you.'

He stiffened. 'I didn't say it did.'

'You didn't have to.'

She lifted her hand, and for a second he thought she was going to touch him. But she stopped, making an awkward gesture instead. A hand spread in front of her body. He grunted.

She studied him, then angled her head and started walking again.

He waited for her to say something. Anything. So he could get angry and cling to the anger instead of this...this stickiness on his skin. This rippling in his blood. It was as if he'd been challenged to a fight and his body was preparing to defend him.

It wouldn't do. It simply wouldn't do.

And *now*, of course, she refused to speak.

'Why aren't you pushing me?' he asked curtly.

'You don't want to talk about your personal life. That's fair. Now,' she said, redirecting their conversation for a third time. 'Let's talk about the mock-up house. Here's what I'm thinking...'

CHAPTER SIX

THE TOWN HALL meeting went better than Morgan had expected. Most of Elliott's team had been stand-offish at first, but once she'd begun to tell them about her plans, divided into specific phases over the next few weeks, she'd seen some of them relax. By the end of it she was sure she had the support, if not the confidence, of most of them.

She knew the confidence would come—as would the support of those she hadn't yet managed to convince. She was good at her job. They would see that and know her participation wasn't a fluke.

Well, they didn't have to know that her participation, especially the way it had come about, actually was a fluke.

The islanders who'd been approached for the construction work had been present during her speech, too. She'd welcomed them, but waited to address them in her plans, wanting Elliott's team to know she was aware of the uneven dynamics. None of the islanders had seemed to mind. They were too grateful for the work and eager to do what needed to be done—including waiting fifteen minutes while she spoke solely to the team.

During those fifteen minutes she'd seen Thad slip into the room. She'd sensed his surprise at seeing her, but she'd ignored it—and him—until she'd turned to the islanders' group. Then she'd given him a slight nod in greeting, and walked the islanders through what would be happening for them in the next few weeks.

When the meeting was done, she struggled not to let her relief and her exhaustion show. There were too many people who'd remained behind...too many people approaching her with questions or comments. She couldn't show them how she was feeling. It would undermine everything she'd worked so hard for. So she sucked it up, and did what she had to do, until there were only two people left.

Thad and Elliott were both leaning against the wall next to the door, so she would have to pass them to leave. It felt like a metaphor of some kind—or not a metaphor, a *punishment*. In punishment for all her awful deeds, the universe had decided to force her to interact with the man she'd nearly slept with and the one she was considering sleeping with.

What?

No. No, she was *not* considering sleeping with Elliott.

She shut down her instinctive response, which was to admire him as he leaned there, looking mouth-wateringly good in jeans and a T-shirt. It seemed to be his uniform, and after seeing him in it so often she thought that it did suit him after all. He didn't need fancy clothing. He drew enough attention simply by being himself.

Morgan!

Right, this was getting embarrassing. She had no idea where it was all coming from, but it could return there without her acknowledgement.

She took a breath and went to deal with her punishment.

'Hey,' she said as a general greeting, and then she looked at Thad. 'How are you?'

'Good,' he answered, offering her a small smile that reminded her of why she'd fallen so hard. 'I didn't expect to see you here.'

'Yeah. I'm taking the lead on the construction work at the estate.'

'Elliott didn't mention it.'

She looked at Elliott. He only offered her a raised brow. It had more of an effect on her than Thad's smile ever had.

'Should he have?' she forced herself to ask Thad.

'No,' Thad said, straightening. 'No reason to, is there?'

He shook his head and put his hands in his pockets. He looked at her, eyes searching her face, before he gave her a half-smile.

'I'll see you around, Morgan.'

He disappeared before she could reply.

Morgan waited a few minutes, then followed. She felt more than saw Elliott's presence as he walked beside her. In silence, they took the same path they had on their way to the Town Hall.

'You haven't seen Thad since you broke up?' he asked.

She'd known he would ask eventually. 'We've seen each other around town over the last decade or so. It usually goes about the same as it just did.'

'He fawns over you.'

It was a comment, not a question, and she laughed before she could help herself. '*Fawns?* Good heavens, Elliott, if that's fawning, then what you've been doing with me is—'

She cut herself off before she could finish that. It was the best thing to do. Especially considering his expression, which had been tight and blank at the beginning of their conversation and was now stormy and blank. Contradictory combinations, but true.

She couldn't read *why* his face was tight or stormy. There was no anger, no frustration, *nothing* behind the surface. Not even the muted expressions she could usually see on him.

It left her feeling frustrated, but that didn't matter. He obviously didn't care whether she could read him or not. If he did, he wouldn't continue to keep his feelings under lock and key. Which was a stupid thing to be angry about. They were his feelings; he could do whatever he wanted with them.

Control them. Mute them. Hide them. Reveal them to her when he shouldn't so she could understand why her relationship with the island mayor ended and why seeing him now was so awkward.

Wait—that last part was about *her*. Although, to be fair, she hadn't told Elliott any of the details about her relationship with Thad. And she never would. She was pretty sure about that.

They were walking in silence now, down Beach Road and through the main town. Without the anxiety of the meeting she could enjoy the surroundings more than she had on their way up. She loved the charm of the town. The sidewalks and its faded paving. The busy shops now that it was the end of the day. The restaurants and café owners and their regular dinner patrons.

She waved back to those who waved. Touched a lamp post every time they passed one. Stared at the benches with their dark brown, almost black wood and their golden plaques with the names of people in town who had donated towards getting them made.

She couldn't remember seeing anything so sentimental in Cape Town. Perhaps in churches, or national gardens, but in a main road of one of the main areas? No.

It was part of what made Penguin Island special. The intimacy of it. The fact that someone could read a name on a bench and someone who lived there would come along and tell them about that person.

'He feels guilty,' Elliott said softly.

It took her a moment to realise he was talking about Thad.

'Neither you nor I live here, but we've come up with a plan to get a significant number of the island's people employed. There are likely people who feel betrayed that their mayor can't help them feed their families. And now that something's being done about it—something that might lead to more employment opportunities down the line—he can look good.' He paused. 'He feels guilty about that, too.'

She angled a look at him. 'He told you that?'

'Some.'

'Liar,' she accused. And when his mouth curved, she laughed. 'But it's very likely true. How astute of you.'

'I have my moments.'

She was about to reply, but he took the wind out of her sails.

'I wanted to say thank you,' he said.

Her head whipped to the side. They'd reached the beach, and he was looking ahead at the waves. She bent down to take off her shoes, used the movement as a moment to compose herself.

'What for?' she asked eventually.

'You could see that I was uncomfortable during our conversation earlier.'

As he was now, she thought.

'You changed the subject, more than once, to account for that.' He cleared his throat. 'So— thank you.'

He gave her a curt nod, then bent to take off his own shoes. She pursed her lips to keep from smiling. But when he straightened she was smiling anyway.

'On a scale from one to ten, how painful was that for you?'

He narrowed his eyes. 'Not nearly as painful as that question.'

She laughed. 'An apology isn't necessary,' she said, sobering. 'Though I appreciate it.' At his questioning look, she clarified. 'I understand your personal life is out of bounds.'

'As long as you also understand that it has nothing to do with you,' he replied stiffly. 'My personal life is complicated.'

'Hmm...'

'Hmm?'

'Hmm,' she confirmed. 'I've researched you, remember? I've seen pictures of all those women on your arm. Maybe it isn't complicated. Maybe *you've* complicated it.'

Something dark lit in his eyes. 'You're jealous?'

'*Jealous?*' She snorted. 'Please. I'm not interested in a man who thinks "fawning" consists of an awkward conversation back and forth.' She'd already walked ahead before she realised he'd stopped. She turned. 'What?'

The darkness was still in his eyes, shimmering right at the surface like a monster in a lake. It was just as dangerous, too, she thought. One wrong move and she'd be snatched and dragged under.

But then he blinked and it disappeared. He began to walk again, ignoring her question.

'You're not the only person with a complicated personal life, you know,' she said after a while.

'You're more open about yours.'

'Am I?' She glanced at him. 'Besides knowing how many members my family consists of—and that I once dated Thad—what do you know about me?'

When he didn't answer, she nodded.

'Exactly.'

For all her talking, she really didn't share details of her life. How had he only noticed that now?

Because he'd thought he knew about her. He'd thought knowing that she had younger siblings, a niece and a grandmother she clearly adored constituted knowing *her*. Same went for her past with the mayor.

But he didn't know what kind of relationship she had with her siblings. She might adore her grandmother but not approve of Edna's fiancé. Thad might have been the love of her life, and something had happened to break them up.

As he looked back on it, he thought the fact that he hadn't noticed had been partly because of her. She talked so cheerfully, so openly and confidently, that simply listening to her drew people in. Created a false sense of intimacy that made them believe she was exactly who she presented herself to be.

But that was a trick. Something to prevent people from looking further. He knew that because he did the same thing. He could see through her facade now. Through that satisfied expression on her face to the pain just beneath.

She *seemed* satisfied that he didn't know her, but she wasn't. Why?

Then she looked at him, narrowed her eyes and stuck out her tongue.

He couldn't remember the last time someone had stuck out a tongue at him. Probably when he'd been a kid. And it sure as hell hadn't had *this* effect on him. Making him acutely aware of his blood, his skin. Both hot, heavy…

He had the sudden impulse to run into the ocean to cool down. It was an inappropriate reaction to someone so silly. Especially after what he'd been thinking. But he'd been completely taken aback by her sticking out her tongue. Not only because of the effect it had had on him, but because it…*charmed* him. Beneath his more sensual physical reaction, something twinkled and sparked. Something he'd never known existed. A lightness that seemed precious. In need of protection.

The strangest part of it all was that it made him want to smile. And that was more dangerous than anything else this woman had made him feel.

'You're upset,' she accused now. 'But you can't get upset because I pointed out something that's true.'

'I'm not upset.'

'You look upset.'

'I'm not upset.'

'You *sound* upset.'

He grunted, and tried to think of something that would stop this back-and-forth. 'You're proud of the fact that I don't know much about you.'

She frowned. 'I wouldn't say "proud".'

'Satisfied?'

'Satisfied,' she agreed after a beat.

Instead of fighting the urge to smile this time, he allowed his lips to lift and found it easier than resistance.

'You're smiling.'

He stopped smiling.

'No!' she moaned. 'No, I'm sorry. I didn't mean to—' She broke off on an exhalation. 'You have a nice smile.'

That lightness exploded in his chest.

He took a breath. 'Thank you.'

Her cheeks lifted as her mouth curved, making her eyes crinkle, but not dimming their sparkle.

She had a nice smile, too.

'Okay, since I'm changing the subject so well these days, let me point out that you also seem satisfied at keeping things from me.'

He couldn't deny that. 'Yes.'

'Why?' she asked. 'Why are we so happy to *not* share things? Surely we should be opening up to people. To be healthy or whatever...'

She kicked out a foot. Sand sprang from her toes and she grinned, absolutely delighted by such a small, simple thing.

His heart skipped.

Just a little—barely noticeable.

He noticed.

'It's too painful,' he answered honestly, surprising himself. 'To talk about things means confronting them. It's easier to ignore them.'

'Is it?' She snorted a little, her joy of only a few moments ago fading. 'I've always told my siblings that ignoring a problem won't make it go away. And I believe that.' She paused. 'I guess I'm a hypocrite, because I ignore my own problems and hope they'll go away.'

'But you don't ignore theirs?'

She angled her head in acknowledgement. Something about it made him want to know more.

'They haven't yet discovered that you don't take your own advice?'

She crossed her arms, hugging her waist as if she were getting cold. But despite the ocean breeze and the time of day it was still warm. There were only a few stragglers on the beach in the distance, and that felt like an injustice.

People deserved summers on Penguin Island. To feel the sun on their skin during the early evening, its heat only a kiss. To see the blue sky mixing with red and orange as if it were an artist's canvas.

People deserved light breezes. To see them fluttering through Morgan's skirt, her hair, making her look like a summer goddess.

He wanted to worship at her feet.

No.

No, he agreed, affirming that cautioning mental voice. She was making him fanciful. Foolish. He didn't do foolish. He did logic, and success, and when it was necessary seduction. As she'd pointed out, he had dated a *lot* of women. They'd all known what to expect, and he'd ensured the experience was pleasurable.

None of them had doubted his abilities beforehand, which made the fact that Morgan did smart a little. He wasn't bad at flirting or seducing. He was just bad at it with *her*.

Which was exactly why seducing her was out of the question.

'No,' Morgan said finally. 'They haven't yet. I don't… I think they don't think about me as a person very often.'

It had taken a long time, and when her answer

had come it had been so soft it might have been carried away by the wind if he hadn't been so attuned to her voice.

She was smiling, but it wasn't one of her bright, sunny smiles. It was a contemplative one. A sad one.

'I didn't mean to make you...' He faltered.

He didn't know what to say. The last time he'd felt so lost had been when he'd gone to see his father in the hospital. Gordon Abel had been sleeping at the time, and it had been disarming to see the man Elliott had sought approval from his entire life looking so weak.

Something had shifted inside Elliott on seeing that, and he'd left the hospital five minutes later.

Before his father could wake up and see him.

Before his mother and brother arrived.

He'd had no desire to spend time with his family when he was feeling so confused.

'It's not you, Elliott,' Morgan said now with a soft sigh. 'I've been ignoring my feelings so long that when they catch up to me I...' She lifted her hands, then shook them in the air as if they were wet.

'You keep absolving me from taking responsibility for things,' he said.

'I do not.'

'You do. It's a kind, innocent thing to do.'

'Innocent?' She stopped walking. Put her hands on her hips. *'Innocent?'*

He stopped walking, too. 'It was meant to be a compliment.'

'Not from you. You mean it's naïve.'

'Not coming from you,' he said. 'Coming from you, it's innocent. I mean it.'

She snorted at him, like a bull letting out a warning, and he almost laughed. But then she began to walk again—stomping, really—and the insidious claws of insecurity gripped him.

Slowly, deliberately, he extricated each one. He'd run away from that feeling with his family, and he wouldn't welcome it back with Morgan.

'Stop,' Morgan said.

He obeyed before he realised her voice had come from behind him; she'd stopped again. He moved towards her, but she lifted a hand.

'No, stay there.' She took a breath. 'I shouldn't have said that. It was rude.'

'You shouldn't have said what?'

'That you saying "innocent" meant naïve. I attribute things to you that I shouldn't. I've done it more than once.'

'Morgan,' he said on a sigh. 'Why does it feel like we're navigating a minefield every time we talk?'

'Do you want the real answer to that? Or the one that's going to keep everything the way it is?'

His heart began to pound, but he said, 'The real answer.'

'Because of the attraction we're ignoring.'

CHAPTER SEVEN

WHAT WAS SHE DOING? *What was she doing?*

The simple answer was something stupid.

She tended to do stupid things when she slowed down enough to listen to her emotions. They made her feel uncomfortable. Made her think about the choices that had brought her to this point in her life. Made her aware of how tired she was of taking care of her family when they hadn't asked her to. Not directly, at least.

'Something stupid' could describe her entire relationship with Thad. And now she was repeating it with Elliott.

'What are you saying?' Elliott asked, that darkness rippling over his face again.

'Nothing.' She shook her head. 'Nothing. Forget what I said.'

'No.'

'No?'

He closed the distance between them. 'No.'

He didn't kiss her, but she knew he was going to. Why else would he be standing so close to her, with barely a whisper between them? She shivered, but it had nothing to do with the weather and everything to do with how aware she was.

Of her body. Of her feet against the sand, the breeze fluttering her skirt, her hair, the mist of the ocean teasing her skin.

Of his body. Of the tips of his toes touching hers, his hands almost trembling at his sides, his eyes intense, aroused, and focused entirely on her.

Of the sun slowly crouching behind the ocean at the horizon.

Of the waves crashing so close to their feet.

Of the privacy they had now that even the last few people at the beach had disappeared.

She tried to remember why stupid was bad. Dangerous. Instead, she said, 'Touch me.'

He obeyed. Slowly he wrapped his arm around her waist. She rested her hands on the biceps she'd admired from a distance, kneading his muscles, feeling a thrilling rush of power because she could. She could smell him—a musky scent mingled with the salty air of the beach—and she closed the distance between them so their bodies were flush.

Now her breasts were pressed against his chest, her stomach against the firmness of his. And at the base of her stomach she felt his hardness against her, too. Heat travelled low, settling between her thighs, making her long to pull him to the ground, push him onto his back and straddle him.

Her eyes lifted. He was still looking at her, with a hooded stare that made her feel hotter. His tongue slipped between his lips, as if he could already taste her there, and her core turned into lava as she imagined what it would be like if he did taste her.

Elliott seemed to agree, because now he was leaning forward. Her lips parted in response and his gaze dipped to it. He leaned even closer...

Then he stopped.

'What?' she choked out.

'You want me to do all the work?' His voice was hoarse, seductive. 'How will I know you want this if you don't take some initiative?'

She pulled his head down and kissed him.

Her stomach swooped. Dropped down to the pits of the earth at the contact. Soft and hot, the kiss was like the feel of a roaring fire after being out in the snow. There was something calming, something reassuring about it even as it heated her. Never before had she been so aroused by a simple meeting of lips. Never before had something so sweet made her body prickle, her nipples harden, her centre ache.

She pulled back in surprise, but his hand slid into her hair and brought her back to his mouth. His other arm still encircled her, pulling her in tightly, securely, and she felt safer than she had in a long time.

Even though she knew she wasn't safe.

Even though she knew what they were doing was dangerous.

He was threatening everything she'd thought she knew, everything she wanted to uphold, and it made no sense for her to feel so…so *right* in his arms.

The thought left her head when his tongue swept into her mouth. He tasted of nothing discernible— and everything she craved. Her arms went around him, pulling him even closer than before. She wanted to be a part of him—no, she wanted him to be a part of *her*.

Another dangerous thought.

An *intimate* thought that came from passion and lust and nothing that she understood.

She loosened her grip on his body but didn't let go. Instead she ran her hands over his body. Over the hard muscle of his back, the broad shoulders and narrow waist. She lingered there, lifting on to her toes so he was positioned between her thighs, then squeezing his butt to bring his hardness to her core.

She shivered as he traced a path over her curves. He stopped at her thigh, digging his fingers into the plushness there before he shifted and rested his hand on her behind. His free hand played with her hair, and his tongue… His tongue played a game with hers. A slow, erotic, pleasurable game that she'd never played before.

It coaxed, it teased, and then he was touching

her hip, her waist, and finally her breast. She moaned in approval, waiting for the wave of desire that would drown her when he teased her nipple, but it didn't come. He'd stopped.

Her eyes popped open. She lowered herself back onto her feet, ready to protest. *Why? Why are you stopping?* But the battle on his face kept her from asking.

When he didn't speak, she asked, 'Are you okay?'

'Me?' He huffed out air in a half-laugh that held no amusement. 'I was about to ask you the same thing.'

'You're the one who stopped.'

'We were about to do something stupid.'

Something stupid.

She stiffened, though she knew he was right. She'd thought it herself, hadn't she? But it was different when he said it. Somehow she'd given him the power to hurt her. So carelessly, too. He'd evaluated the situation—*her*—and thought it was stupid.

No, that wasn't true. She was deliberately misunderstanding him. But it didn't matter. A little balloon of hurt had still popped in her chest, stealing her breath, leaving her feeling...

Alone.

The feeling echoed in her mind, in her body, and its intensity told her that it didn't only apply to her situation with Elliott. She felt alone in her family, too. She'd never thought it before, never given herself the chance to feel it. But it was true, and she closed her eyes, letting the pain of realisation wash over her before she squared her shoulders and faced Elliott.

'I didn't mean to upset you,' he said slowly.

She could hear the angst in his voice and it softened her. 'You haven't upset me. I *am* upset, but it isn't you.' *Not only you, at least.* 'You were right to stop. This… It shouldn't have happened. You're right.' She blew out a breath. 'If my grandmother asks, I'm late because we wanted a debrief after the meeting.'

'She'll ask?' Elliott frowned. 'No. Surely not.'

'She will,' Morgan said with certainty. 'But on the off-chance that she doesn't, let's stagger our return and hope my grandmother has learnt to respect boundaries since I last saw her. Doubtful, but what's life without hope?'

Ignoring all the ways they'd managed to complicate their relationship in less than thirty minutes, Morgan began to walk back to the estate.

'Oi, you!'

Elliott stopped. He recognised the voice, but it couldn't be addressing him. Edna Smith hadn't once called him by saying, *Oi, you!* Still, he stopped. Turned. Saw her storming towards him.

It shouldn't have been as intimidating as it was.

But he knew that Morgan's warning was about to come to fruition.

Mentally, he tried to prepare.

And failed.

'What did you do to my granddaughter?'

He opened his mouth to recite the words Morgan had told him to say, but stopped when he realised they wouldn't fit.

He tried to adjust. 'I'm not sure what you mean.'

'I'll clarify,' she told him, almost kindly, but he didn't miss the sharpness that was present, too. 'Morgan came home later than I expected from the Town Hall. When I asked her about it, she refused to tell me the truth.'

'But she did tell you something?' he asked.

Edna nodded.

'How do you know it wasn't the truth?'

'She said you wanted a debrief after the meeting.'

'Yes.'

'She looked too shaken up for that to be true. Why did she look shaken up?'

Because I messed things up.

To Edna, he said, 'The meeting was taxing.'

'I thought it went well.'

'It did. But it was trying for her. She was nervous about getting my team's support, and the islanders' respect.'

Edna harrumphed. 'They respect her.'

'As an employer?'

'*You're* their employer.'

He tilted his head. 'I believe that's the kind of thinking that she was nervous about.'

Edna narrowed her eyes, but there was no retort. He nodded, satisfied that he'd made his point, and waited until she figured out how she wanted to harass him next. What he really wanted to do was leave and do what he had come to the estate to do: check on Morgan's progress with the mock-up house. But leaving would be rude, and he wouldn't insult Morgan's grandmother that way.

Except it wasn't only Morgan's grandmother. Behind Edna was Joyce, Edna's best friend, and behind Joyce her other friends, Clarice and Sharon.

An involuntary shudder went down Elliott's spine. He'd only met them once, but that had been enough. Now he avoided them whenever he could.

He had no idea how he'd got himself into this situation.

Because you wanted to see Morgan.

He didn't need to be on site today. Morgan had assured him she had things handled. But he wanted to show her that he trusted her. He wanted to show everyone else that, too. Besides, he had his own company to run. He'd chosen a great team who could manage without his physical presence, but he still had emails to work through and virtual meetings to attend. And he needed to do that now, while he wasn't needed at the estate.

But he *wanted* to see her. To assure himself that he'd blown their chemistry out of proportion. Everything that had happened the day before must have been a fluke—especially that kiss.

That *phenomenal* kiss.

He had never in his life experienced intimacy so potent. It had only been a kiss, but he'd wanted to tear her clothes off. More worryingly, that kiss had made him think about more than just a physical relationship. Which made coming to see her now a stupid thing to do.

'Leave him alone,' Joyce said mildly. 'He clearly doesn't want to tell you anything.'

Wisely, he didn't comment on that.

'But I'll tell you,' Joyce went on.

'You will?' both he and Edna asked.

'They kissed,' Clarice said. 'Joyce told us earlier.'

'*I* wanted to tell them,' Joyce almost growled.

'I could tell you were going to make it a whole thing and it was just going to drag out,' Clarice told her. 'So, *did* you kiss?'

That last part was addressed to him. But why was Clarice asking for confirmation when Joyce already sounded so confident? It might have nothing to do with him. Maybe Clarice simply didn't trust Joyce to tell the truth and was looking for confirmation. But that was unlikely. What *was* likely was that someone had told Joyce they thought they'd seen Morgan and Elliott on the beach, kissing, but they couldn't be sure, and now they were looking to him to respond.

All of this was his own speculation, which he would never voice out loud because it would give them exactly what they wanted.

'Why are you convinced Morgan's state has something to do with me?' he asked instead.

Sharon shrugged. 'Who else would it be?'

'Thad? He was at the Town Hall last night.'

Edna gaped at him. 'She *told* you about Thad?'

Uneasiness crept over him. 'Yes. Why?'

'She hasn't told anyone about Thad. Not even me.'

'But—' He took a moment to recalibrate. 'How did you know what I meant, then?'

'Oh, that girl was Frenching our mayor all over town that summer,' Sharon said, rolling her eyes. 'She thought she was being covert, but she wasn't. She's actually really bad at it.'

'Which is how we know you two kissed,' Joyce interjected.

She studied him, still waiting for him to confirm. His lips twitched, but he managed to keep them in a line, refusing to give in to the feeling of amusement that had come at her attempt at trickery.

'You don't know for sure what upset her, then?'

he asked lightly, though it wasn't really a question. 'I think I'll take my leave.'

He nodded a greeting, then began to walk back to his house. He couldn't go to the mock-up house now—not with those women watching him. They'd probably follow him, peppering him with questions he didn't want to answer.

Questions he *couldn't* answer.

He *was* the reason Morgan was, as her grandmother had put it, 'shaken'. And it shamed him. Angered him. He was becoming too invested in Morgan. Now he wanted to go and see her to make amends for… For whatever it was called when a kiss rocked the very foundation of a professional relationship.

And now he had to worry because he'd told Edna and her friends about Morgan and Thad. There was likely a reason she hadn't told them. But why had she told *him*? Surely that meant she was feeling the connection between them, too? She must be; she'd been the one to bring up their attraction in the first place…

This was precisely why he hated personal relationships.

He'd spent almost half his life feeling this kind of uncertainty. His parents had never quite adored him as much as they had Gio. He'd done whatever he could to try and get them to. But nothing he did had been enough. He'd seen that early on, and still he'd tried. Always hoping that maybe this time they'd see him. Really see him. But that hope had been futile, and it had come with the anxiety of wondering if *this* would be the moment he'd been waiting for. The anxiety of wondering if he was doing enough.

It had taken their non-reaction at him getting into the best university in the country on a full scholarship to realise that nothing he could do would ever be enough for them. Not when Gio was the standard to live up to.

So he'd started creating his own standards. Started focusing on the things he could control—unlike his parents' affection and pride. He'd chosen each relationship with care from then on, never getting close to anyone so he'd never again have to flounder as he had with his parents.

Morgan was threatening all of that—and he wouldn't allow it.

CHAPTER EIGHT

MORGAN TRIED NOT to be annoyed. Yes, she had told Elliott that the mock-up house was almost complete. Yes, she'd expected him to see it in person. But she hadn't explicitly *told* him to come, and she shouldn't expect him to read her mind.

She still did. Because her expectations when it came to him were unreasonably high. She didn't know why—and she didn't like it. Having high expectations almost always led to disappointment. She had experienced that over and over again, growing up. She'd managed to set them aside, realising that they hurt more than helped when it came to her parents.

Don't think about it, she told herself, but it was too late. A wave of memories had already washed over her.

Her mother crying on the phone to Grandma Edna, asking for help with Morgan. Her father standing in the corner, looking helpless and angry.

Her mother shaking her head at the end of the

call. 'She says she can come for a while, but it's not a permanent solution.'

'Why not?' her father had barked.

'Because she lives on an island! Because we're Morgan's parents, not her!'

'So let Morgan live with her on her island.'

Her mother had disagreed. 'We can't do that. We *are* Morgan's parents.'

'What's that going to matter if we can't take care of her?'

Her father had pushed away from the counter, stormed out of the kitchen, and Morgan had run from her hiding place in the passage to her bed. She'd been there barely a minute when her mother had come in and cuddled her.

She'd been three at the time. She should have been too young to remember it so vividly. But perhaps it was so vivid because of the vow she'd made to herself that day, as her mother's arms came around her.

Morgan had promised herself she would do everything in her power to make sure taking care of her would be easy for her parents. She'd entertain herself when her parents had to study for their exams, she'd eat whatever she was given, even if it made her stomach hurt, and she'd be the best damn daughter any person could ask for.

And she had been.

Things had become easier a year or so after that conversation. Grandma Edna had made some calls and got Morgan's father a stable job at a shoe factory, where he'd quickly climbed the ranks. Morgan's mother had finished school and received a scholarship to study full time, but had got a job anyway.

By the time Hattie had come along the financial situation hadn't been as dire and her parents had been less stressed, although they'd still been young and trying to get their lives back on the track having Morgan had diverted them from. And so Morgan had helped with Hattie, and then with her brother Rob, and things had been a lot easier for everyone.

Or so she'd told herself. Because at some point she'd stopped expecting her parents to tell her she no longer had to be Hattie and Rob's third parent. Or her own parent, for that matter.

She exhaled. Shook her shoulders. Tilted her head from side to side to stretch out the muscles.

'Preparing for a fight?' a soft voice asked from behind her. 'I come in peace, I assure you.'

How could something as simple as his voice make her feel so prickly? And then she turned, and her stomach swooped again almost as intensely as it had when their lips had touched three days before.

Three days. This man had waited three days before coming to see her.

She had no right to feel betrayed, but she did.

She had no right to expect anything from him—and *he* had no right to have this effect on her.

He wore his uniform of T-shirt and jeans again, and this time the shirt was white. It made the brown of his skin look rich, full. It clung to his arms, his chest, his torso, and highlighted his strength.

Or maybe she only felt that way because she'd felt his body. Run her hands over those arms, that chest. She hadn't had the luxury of touching him everywhere yet, not in the way she wanted to.

She took a breath and let it out slowly.

Yes, Elliott was attractive, and she was attracted to him. But her reaction was unreasonable. She needed to control herself.

'I didn't see you there,' she said in a measured voice. 'It's been a long day and I was trying to stretch out my muscles.'

The lie slid smoothly from her tongue. Despite it, she thought Elliott knew the truth. His gaze was intent on her, searching. Then it abruptly shifted, taking in the room behind her.

This one had been one of the easier ones to fix, which was why she'd chosen it as the mock-up house. The biggest problem had been some holes in the walls, but those had been easily plastered. The rest of the changes had been superficial.

The walls of each room had now been painted in a shade of white, beige or blue, which matched the handwoven rugs on the floor. The dining and coffee tables were both a light-coloured wood, beautiful and natural—courtesy of "Crafted."

She hadn't asked, but Elliott had offered his company's services and these had been the first pieces to arrive. Along with a ladder shelf that she'd decorated with books and plants, they tied everything in the room they were currently in together.

There were other things she'd added—paintings on the walls in the living room, flowers in the kitchen, candles and cushions in the bedrooms—but those were minor, their purpose to round out the rooms. She'd worked with the interior designer on Elliott's team, and she thought the outcome was close to what Abel and Son Development had wanted when they'd first hired the designer. Morgan had run everything by Elliott, and she'd been feeling pretty confident about it all.

But that confidence was slowly dissipating with each passing second of silence. Part of her was offended. She hadn't expected him to drop to his knees in awe, but *some* reaction would have been better than nothing.

There you go, expecting again.

As annoying as it was, that voice in her head was right. In this situation especially, where Elliott was essentially playing the role of her boss, she needed to have no expectations at all and accept his response. Although that was not very realistic, because even with paying clients she had expectations. She followed their brief, checked in with them multiple times during the process, and she expected them to like what she did. So maybe she was overreacting.

Or maybe he's broken your brain.

This was exactly why she avoided relationships. They took up too much mental space, too much emotional space, and she had enough of her own baggage to fill up those spaces.

'It's amazing,' Elliott said, saving her from that thought.

'Yeah?' She exhaled in relief, as if she hadn't just told herself to get a grip. 'You like it?'

'It's amazing,' he repeated. 'It looks modern, yet somehow retains the traditional feel of the estate.'

'I've kept some of the original pieces.' She pointed out the paintings, the carpet, a throw. 'Minor, but they have enough personality to influence the room. Plus, your furniture is gorgeous. If you could have a few pieces in each of the houses and things pick up, it'll drive a lot of business to Crafted.'

He angled his head slightly, a frown knitting his brow.

'It's worth considering,' she said. 'These houses are going to act like the best showrooms. People will be able to see your pieces in a home setting, interact with them… Think about how often people hesitate over buying something like a chair because they're unsure of its quality. And if they're impressed—which, of course, they will be—they'll buy from you. The best showroom,' she said again. 'Although maybe the costliest, too.'

'I'm not worried about that.'

'Of course not, Mr Tycoon,' she said, rolling her eyes. Then she took a proper look at him. 'You're worried about something else?'

He clenched his jaw, then relaxed it. 'It's fine.'

When he didn't offer more information, she sighed. 'I don't know why I still try.' At his questioning look, she shook her head. 'Forget it.'

'No.'

'Are you sure?' she asked mildly. 'Because you're not going to like it when I elaborate.'

He simply watched her.

She took it as a sign to continue.

'I get it. You're private.'

'As are you,' he interjected. 'We've covered that, haven't we?'

'I'd be a little less private if you were too.' She shrugged. 'That minefield you talked about? This is a part of it. There are so many things we can't talk about. I feel like an explosion might go off at any moment during our conversations.'

'You'd prefer us to be more open about our lives?'

'I'm not asking you to give me your entire history. Just…' She trailed off. 'No, it's fine. I'm sorry. I shouldn't have… There are things in my life I don't want to talk about either. Forget I said anything.'

He folded his arms. Studied her.

She did everything in her power not to shift. Not to show him how disturbing it was to have the intensity in his eyes directed at her so completely.

'I don't know if my father and brother would allow my furniture in the houses,' he said, shifting his gaze.

She almost sagged at the reprieve.

'And I don't know if I want to ask.'

'Why not?' she asked.

When he looked at her this time his expression wasn't muted. It was sad. Angry. Embarrassed. There were a multitude of emotions she couldn't read, too. She only felt them deep in her chest. Her heart ached. At *him*; at his vulnerability. It was as if he had confessed his deepest, most protected secret.

Maybe he has.

She blew out a breath—stealthily, she hoped, because she didn't want him to think he was affecting her. And she didn't want him to feel bad about it.

'The dynamics in my family aren't easy,' he said carefully. 'If I ask, there's no guarantee they'll say yes.'

And so he wouldn't ask, she realised, and wondered what they'd done to make him feel this way.

'I'm sorry,' she said softly. 'If it makes you feel any better…'

'Yes?'

'No, I've got nothing.'

He stared.

She wrinkled her nose. 'That's pretty ridiculous, Elliott. My family is tough, too, but I'm pretty sure they'd help me with my business if I asked.'

'Morgan…'

He looked so offended that she laughed. And then she couldn't stop laughing. Because his family was ridiculous, and the fact that she'd told him that was even more ridiculous. She hadn't said anything remotely comforting when she really should have.

That sobered her right up.

'I'm sorry,' she said. 'No wonder you didn't want to tell me. I handled that horribly.'

But he was smiling.

The first time he'd smiled it had been nice. A small smile—one he hadn't even noticed he'd been giving. Now he was fully present. Now his smile was wide, genuine, disarming. It changed his face from scarily handsome to unbelievably handsome. Softened the frown lines; curved the usually straight lips.

If she were a warrior princess in need of a deadly weapon, she'd take him along with her and tell him to smile in front of all her enemies.

'You handled it fine,' he told her gruffly, the smile fading.

It was like the sun going down on a cold day, leaving only ice behind.

'It affirmed something I thought was only in my head,' he said.

'I can't be the first person who's done that.'

'You're the first person I've told,' he said simply.

It wasn't simple. It was significant. Hugely significant. It added another layer to their relationship. Another complicated, confusing layer that would no doubt take up a lot of Morgan's time and energy as she tried to figure it out.

Oddly, she didn't mind. Not in that moment, anyway. In that moment she could only think about how honoured she was that he'd share something so deeply personal with her. He *had* told her a secret, and it was one he hadn't told anyone else.

But she couldn't show him that. If she did, she'd be making a big deal of it—and that would be the last thing he'd want. It would be the last time he told her anything, too. So she'd joke.

'Do you want me to kill them?' she asked.

'What?'

'You heard me,' she said, feigning seriousness. 'I'm good at solving problems. I can make your family disappear like *that*.' She snapped her fingers. 'Just say the word.'

His lips parted, brow furrowed, and he regarded her in silence with a faint look of suspicion on his face.

She snorted. 'It's a joke, Elliott. I'm joking. I am not a murderer, nor can I order hits on people.' She narrowed her eyes. 'Unless that's what you want me to do?'

This time she laughed at his expression. Because he was annoyed by her, but he was also amused—and he didn't know what to do about either. Seconds later, though, he shocked her by laughing, too. A soft, deep chuckle that had her skin turning to gooseflesh. She grinned so hard she felt as if she'd been turned into stone with a smile on her face.

When he stopped laughing, he returned her smile. A slight curve of his lips, nowhere near the smile of earlier, but her heart flipped.

'Thank you,' he said, shoving his hands into his pockets. 'I needed that.'

'You're very welcome.'

In her head she played around with what she wanted to say next. Decided to go for it even if it affected the easiness that had settled between them.

'They don't have to know. About the Crafted pieces, I mean. If you really want to do this we'll sneak in the furniture.'

'I don't "sneak".'

'Oh, I know. Crafted is a big, well-established

company. It doesn't deserve to be sneaked in, blah-blah-blah.' She said it lightly, hoping he'd understand where she was coming from. 'I just meant that if you wanted to do it we can, and your family doesn't have to know.' She looked around. 'Do they know about these pieces?'

'No, but they were donations. If we did this in all the houses Abel and Son Development would have to buy the furniture. Which makes "sneaking" nearly impossible,' he added dryly.

'So, donate more.'

'I can't donate what it would take to furnish an entire estate.'

'Why not?'

'My board of directors would have something to say about that.'

'They didn't have anything to say about these pieces?'

'Too few pieces to care about.'

Her eyes narrowed. 'You're lying…'

He frowned. 'They don't care about a few pieces of furniture.'

'I'm sure that's true, but I don't think it's relevant in this particular conversation.'

'You can't possibly—'

'*You* donated them,' she interrupted. 'You own these pieces, don't you?'

He exhaled sharply. 'Fine. Yes. They're mine. I bought them.'

'You bought your own pieces?' she repeated thoughtfully. 'For this house?'

'No.' He looked to the sky, then back at her. 'I've been buying pieces since the inception of the company. It…motivates me. Every time we make a significant sale, I buy something. If the sale is big, I buy something big. If it's small, I buy something small.'

'So you have a warehouse full of your own company's furniture?'

He nodded stiffly. And was that…? Was that a blush on his cheeks? It was! The faintest pink against his brown skin.

Instead of teasing him about it—it would be cruel to make fun of him when he was embarrassed, though it was hard to resist—she said, 'Mine's decorating.'

'Your what is decorating?'

'My reward, I guess. For making my company a success. My house is pretty empty. Deliberately. I bought this big old house that was essentially a blank canvas. The roof was leaking when I first got it, the paint was peeling in most of the rooms, and the tiles were cracked. But the plumbing was intact, the water pressure was amazing, and the kitchen was big and modernised. I have no idea why,' she added, 'considering the rest of the place was a mess. But when I first saw it I knew it was mine. So I bought this broken house and I've been fixing it up ever since.'

'You literally live with the success of your career?'

'No, I live in a disaster area.'

'Surely your house is complete by now?'

'I appreciate your confidence in the success of my company, but I've only just managed to fix the walls, repaint them, and retile. The roof wasn't part of my deal with myself—the leaking was excessive, and it would have ruined whatever I did in the house anyway—so I had that done before I moved in. The rest will take time.'

'But your company *is* successful.'

'I'm doing the renovations myself. What I *can* do, anyway. The tiling I've had to outsource, but I can replaster walls and paint, and I did those things first. My bedroom is pretty perfect, because I sank a lot of my attention into it, but the rest… It needs more time, and I don't always have it.'

'Why not?'

She'd braced herself for the question, and since he'd been honest with her she said, 'I spend a lot of time with my family. I help my younger sister take care of my niece. And my younger brother is still at university. He sometimes needs help with his assignments because of a learning disability.'

'I'm sorry,' he said softly. He must have seen her confusion, because he continued, 'Your parents? I didn't realise they'd passed away.'

'What? Oh, no. No, they're alive.'

'Then why—?'

A knock cut him off. Elliott looked at her questioningly, but she shook her head and shrugged.

He strode to the door then, opened it—and she saw his jaw drop. Her feet were already moving, her brain urging them forward, since Elliott never showed that much emotion so easily and it must have been an emergency.

She nudged him and he stepped back, and her own jaw dropped.

Because in front of them were roses.

Rows and rows of roses.

CHAPTER NINE

HE WAS BEING FRAMED—and it didn't take a genius to figure out by whom.

Elliott was mildly horrified at the number of flowers in the garden. How had Edna and her friends even managed to find so many roses on the island? They'd filled the small front yard, leaving only the path free. Morgan would have to walk through the roses to get to the road—which was, he would admit, romantic. But he hadn't had anything to do with it.

Morgan seemed to realise it, too.

Her bemused expression quickly changed to humour, and then she turned to him, grinning. 'I told you.'

'Told me what?'

'My grandmother.' Morgan put her hands on her hips, staring at the flowers again. 'She can't help herself.' With a shake of her head, she looked over her shoulder. 'What did you do?'

'I don't know… She ambushed me, like you

said she would, but I didn't tell her anything you and I didn't agree on.'

He thought back to the conversation and winced. It was too much to expect her not to notice.

'What?' she asked.

'I…' He swallowed. The nerves tangled with his tongue, and it took him longer than he would have liked to answer. 'She said you were upset after the Town Hall meeting, and I might have implied that the reason for it was Thad's presence.'

She faced him now, her usually cheerful expression neutral. 'Implied?'

He sighed. 'Said. Outright.'

'You told my grandmother that I was upset because of Thad?' She didn't wait for his confirmation. 'You decided to shift the blame off yourself by telling them about my ex-boyfriend, whom I have personally never told her about?'

'In my defence,' he said weakly, 'I didn't realise she didn't know about Thad. Or rather, that you hadn't told her.'

'What does that mean?'

'They all knew. Your grandmother and her friends,' he clarified. 'You're very bad at sneaking around. Apparently.'

'My grandmother *and* her friends?' She snorted. 'You *were* ambushed.'

'Yes.'

'Don't sound so relieved. You're not off the hook yet.'

But she was smiling. At him. He had never experienced something so warm and light as her teasing. Or something as precious and as pure as her opening up to him. *He* was responsible for that. He'd let her into his head, his hurt, just a fraction, and she'd trusted him in return.

It felt too impossible to be real. Too *good* to be real. His actions were progressing a relationship with someone he actually cared about. That had never happened before—largely because he'd never allowed it to. Not after his actions had done nothing to change things with his parents. But they were changing things now, with Morgan, and it made him feel…hopeful.

The very thought had tension thrumming in his veins.

He ignored it and watched as Morgan stepped off the veranda onto the path, lowering herself to her haunches and playing with the petals of one of the flowers.

'I know this isn't real, but it's beautiful,' she said softly.

The soft undertone of disappointment made him desperately wish it *was* real. 'I'm sorry.'

She straightened. 'Don't be.' Then she tilted her head. 'You didn't tell them about what happened between us?'

'Of course not. But—'

'But…?'

'Joyce seemed to know that we…' He trailed off. Cleared his throat. 'Kissed.'

'What?'

'I have no idea how she knew, but she told me—well, actually, Sharon told me. Or was it Clarice?' He shook his head. 'The point is, they had the information. Which I did not confirm.'

She pursed her lips. 'So, they heard a rumour that we kissed, confronted you, and you told them about Thad, which I hadn't told them about.' She heaved out a breath. 'They want us to be together.' He shook his head. She lifted her brow. 'Really? You don't see that in all of this?' She waved her hand over the flowers.

'Perhaps it was meant to be a simple gesture.'

'Oh, no. Those women do not do "simple". I bet you they're planning our wedding, because they think we've had both a physical connection because of the kiss and an emotional connection because I confided in you about Thad. We'd better be careful. They'll be watching us.'

'No, they won't,' he managed to say over the intense desire to ask her if they did, indeed, have a physical and emotional connection.

'Hmm… You're right. They probably sent one of the neighbourhood kids to ring the doorbell.' She looked around. 'They wouldn't dare show their faces now. Too worried we might murder them. And even if they did show,' she continued with a huff of air, 'they'd hunch their backs over, walk really slowly, and make themselves seem like innocent old ladies. But the joke's on them! We all know that isn't true.'

He stared. 'They *do* that?'

'Oh, you sweet summer child. Yes, they do. It's a ploy to make you feel bad for not doing something they want you to do. It's fool-proof, too. You can't trust it, but you'd be a terrible person to ignore it on the off-chance that it *is* true.'

Now that the surprise had worn off, Elliott remembered that he'd already been victim to that ploy. Edna had done it after their first meeting. She'd risen from her chair slowly, as if her body was aching, and walked back to her car taking double the time he now knew she needed.

He should be upset about it—and the multiple other times she had manipulated him—but he wasn't. In fact, he felt reluctant amusement.

'They grow on you,' Morgan said with a soft sigh. 'You realise they have good intentions, so even when you're mad at them you're okay with being swept into one of their houses and handed a fresh batch of biscuits.'

'Biscuits would have been preferable.'

She smiled. 'So boring, though. And less aesthetically appealing, for sure.'

He walked down the steps but didn't breach the space between them. She was looking at the flowers again. There was a light flush of pleasure on her cheeks, and again he wished that he *had* done this for her.

He wished he hadn't spoiled their kiss with his careless words. He'd thought about it after his encounter with Edna, and now he saw that maybe Morgan hadn't been upset by the kiss itself, but by the way he'd handled it.

He had to apologise.

He cleared his throat. 'The other day,' he started. 'On the beach…'

She looked at him, eyebrows raised.

'The kiss,' he clarified.

'Yes?'

'I didn't think it was stupid.'

'You said it, though.'

'Well, it *was* a stupid thing for us to do. There should be boundaries we don't cross. This project is important and…'

He trailed off. Was he really going to do this? *Say* this? He continued before he knew it, because she was looking at him with soft brown eyes and she had a power over him he would never understand.

'It wasn't stupid for me to kiss you.'

'I can't tell what the difference is.' Her voice was low. Husky.

'You can.'

She pressed her tongue into her cheek. 'Hmm…'

He took a tentative step closer. When she didn't move away, he took another step. There was barely a breath between them now, but again she didn't walk away. She only lifted her eyes, challenge, curiosity, interest clear in her gaze.

'I don't take risks in my personal life, Morgan. I don't like feeling...' *Unwanted.* 'Vulnerable.' Both were true, anyway. 'I don't have experience with relationships. Real ones,' he added, since she'd already brought up the women he'd dated. 'Everything about this feels real. Too real,' he said with a frown.

A piece of her hair fluttered over her forehead. He focused on that. The slight curl of it... the tiniest fuzz around its edges. Slowly, he lifted his hand, gripped the strands between his index finger and thumb, and gently put it back behind her ear. It promptly flew to the front again. He smiled.

'When you say things like that...when you do things like this...' She nodded her head, so he'd know she was talking about his actions with her hair. 'You take my breath away.' Her hands gripped the front of his T-shirt. 'I don't like feeling vulnerable either. The last time a man made me feel that way I almost lost...' Her voice faded. Her fingers tightened.

'I don't want you to lose anything,' he whispered.

'I know.' Her gaze met his. 'Maybe that's why I feel like I'm gaining something with you instead.'

His heart filled. Overflowed. With what, he

didn't know. He wasn't sure he wanted to find out. But he knew that honesty had brought them here. Vulnerability. Things he'd viewed as enemies since they'd done nothing but hurt him when he'd tried them with his family.

But they'd brought him this closeness with Morgan. Literally and figuratively. Both seemed of the utmost importance. Although literal closeness took precedence now, because he could see the faint dusting of freckles on her right cheek. There were none on her left, and it fascinated him. As did the sparkle in her eyes. Every time he looked at them he came up with a better description for their colour. Today they looked mahogany. Full, deep, rich...

The colour would make the most beautiful piece of furniture. A desk, he thought. He'd make a desk of this exact colour so that he could be reminded of her eyes, of her, whenever he sat down to work.

'What are you thinking about?' she asked quietly.

His eyes dipped to her lips. They were somewhere between pink and red, reminding him of a tart fruit, and their creases formed a pattern he wanted to memorise. An impossible task. An illogical task. He wanted to take it on, nevertheless.

'I'm thinking I'd... I'd like to kiss you.'

She smiled. 'What are you waiting for?'

He immediately lowered his head and kissed

her. Drank her in as if she was a potion that would give him eternal happiness. He savoured it. The taste of her tongue…the feel of it teasing his. Heat scattered through his body, sending nerves prickling as she deepened the kiss.

His hands settled at her waist, his fingers digging into her skin.

Touching.

Claiming.

Wanting.

She groaned, pulled him in closer, her hands fisting his shirt before they moved to his stomach. His muscles tensed beneath her warmth, beneath her exploration, and for a moment he lost his breath. He pulled away, chest heaving, and she blinked up at him.

'Too much?'

'Not enough,' he growled, and lifted her.

Her legs went around his waist, her mouth fused with his, and he walked up the steps, back through the door. Or he tried to. He got up to the second step and his foot caught, and then they went tumbling down to the ground.

He angled his body to shield her from the worst of it. The good news was that it worked: she landed on him. The bad news was that he took the impact from her and from the ground. His breath was stunned out of him, and it took him a long while before he could respond to her panicked words.

'Elliott? *Elliott?* Are you okay?' She was kneeling next to him, frantically patting his body—he assumed to check for injuries.

'Morgan,' he managed. 'You're touching me.'

'Of course I'm touching you. I'm checking for—' She stopped, before catching his face between her hands. 'You're talking! That means you're okay, right? I didn't kill you?'

He huffed out a laugh, pushing himself up as he did so. 'You didn't kill me. Only my pride has died.'

'*Your* pride?' she asked. 'I'm the one who made you fall.'

'No, my foot caught.'

Come to think of it, his ankle felt a little unpleasant. He lowered it to check on it, felt a twinge in his back, too.

He groaned. 'Clearly not in my twenties any more,' he muttered.

'You're not?' She blinked. 'If I'd known that, I probably wouldn't have made out with you.'

He opened his mouth, even though he didn't know what he was going to say. But she rolled her eyes and gave a small laugh.

'Don't look so concerned. It was a joke. Now, put your arm around my shoulders and let me help you up.'

He obeyed, wincing a little when he put weight on his ankle.

'We need to get you to a doctor.'

'No,' he said. 'I can feel it isn't that bad. I just need to ice it.'

She didn't look convinced, but she merely said, 'I'm assuming you walked here?' At his nod, she pointed to a green car in the driveway. 'That's mine. I'll take you home, get you what you need, and then leave you to languish in the not so bad-ness of yourself.'

Despite the pain, he snorted.

Didn't that seem to be the general gist of his experience with Morgan?

CHAPTER TEN

MORGAN HELPED ELLIOTT to his couch, and only then did she allow herself to look around.

Old Mr Barnaby had lived in this house when she was growing up. He'd been a sour man who'd hated children. To him, 'child' had referred to anyone under eighteen, so Morgan had never really interacted with him.

He'd died by the time she hit her early twenties, and the house on the hill that she'd personally believed to be haunted had stood empty.

By the time she'd become an adult, settled in her career and able to appreciate the beauty of its structure, the house had been bought. No one knew by whom, as still the house had sat empty. When the *For Sale* sign had finally disappeared Edna had called Morgan, speaking in excited tones about the possibility of someone new moving to the island.

Of course that excitement had faded once they'd discovered the house had been bought by property developers—Elliott's family, not Elliott, so she felt less bad about judging it.

There was a part of Morgan that had thought the house would be a ruin. Mr Barnaby hadn't exactly seemed the type of person to keep things clean and tidy. Besides, the house had sat empty for years.

She had been wrong.

The house was sleek and modern. Natural light streamed through the windows and glass doors, reflected by the white tiles, white walls, the white roof with its wooden panels.

The couch in the living room faced one of the glass doors, overlooking the ocean, and to its left was an electric fireplace. To its right, furniture had been arranged to form a dining room with the most gorgeous table she had ever seen. It was large, oak, and had three chairs on one side, a bench on the other, and chairs at both heads of the table.

She resisted the temptation to examine it, and instead looked at the kitchen, just beyond the dining area. It was white, again, though the appliances—all top of the line; she could tell by how complicated they looked—were black.

There were two staircases on either side of the front door, both leading to upper passages with a glass railing that overlooked the open area below. She could see three or so doors on each side, and imagined they disappeared into modern bedrooms.

She turned to him. 'This is going to be a problem.'

'What is?'

'Getting you up those stairs.'

'There's an elevator.' He tilted his head to one side, where she saw a hidden door she now knew to be an elevator. 'Goes directly to the master bedroom.'

'Wow.' She plopped down onto the couch beside him. 'This is some house, huh?'

He shrugged. 'Do you like it?'

She looked around again. 'It's…nice.'

'Nice?' he repeated with a grim smile. 'Small word, so much meaning.'

She snorted. 'No, I mean it. It's nice.'

He merely looked at her.

'But,' she continued with a roll of her eyes, 'it feels cold. I think that's because the man who used to live here kidnapped children from town and ate them, so I guess my opinion comes with baggage.'

He stared for a second, shook his head. 'Sometimes it's hard to know when you're being sincere.'

'I'm sorry.' She thought about it and winced. 'My mother hates it. I don't do it often, but when I do, I really lean in.'

'You do do it often.'

'With you, yes. And, no, I don't know what that means.'

His lips curved. It seemed to come easier now. Because of her? she wondered.

Yeah, yeah, she knew she was crossing a line. She didn't need the cautionary voice in her head to tell her so.

'I like it.'

Listening to that cautionary voice now, she didn't climb onto his lap and begin purring. Instead she made a sound of acknowledgement and looked out of the window. It was evening, with the sky shifting from light blue to navy, the ocean dark but still visible.

'Do *you* like the house?' she asked softly.

'No.' His answer came quickly. 'It reminds me of—' He exhaled abruptly. 'It used to feel cold in my house when I was growing up, too.'

It had clearly been difficult for him to say.

'I'm sorry,' she offered.

'Don't be. It's done.'

'But it's not.' She took his hand. 'It's never really done, is it? My…' She hesitated, then told herself it was too late to hold back. 'My house now is the opposite of what I grew up in. It's… calm. I know that's a strange way to describe a house, but—'

'I understand.' He tightened his grip on her fingers. 'Your life sounds busy. Helping your siblings.'

'Busy. Chaotic. More so when I was growing up because I was so young.'

'Where were your parents?'

'They had me when they were teenagers,' she said with a light snort. 'It became almost natural for me to step in when they needed me to.'

She'd just told herself it was too late to hold back, but she was still doing it. To protect herself, she realised. Not so much from Elliott—although that was certainly a factor, and one she didn't think she could manage to think about right now—she was protecting herself *from* herself. If she told him the truth, what she'd buried in a hole deep inside her would come out. She wasn't ready for that.

'If you're looking to make a place that doesn't feel like your house growing up, it's an easy fix.'

His frown deepened, but he didn't push. In fact, he indulged her. 'Tell me.'

'Make the place feel warmer. Furniture would be an excellent start. Get some Crafted pieces.' She paused. 'Do you know how often I use Crafted for my clients?'

'Really?'

'Really,' she said, looking around. 'I've used other furniture providers, too, but it doesn't feel the same.'

She looked at him and saw something burn in his gaze. She quickly turned away.

'Then I'd recommend painting the walls.

Maybe even the ceiling. No, those wooden panels look gorgeous against the white. Leave that. But definitely paint these.' She pointed to the walls. 'If you change them from white to, say, a cream or a beige—something softer—it'll help things seem less harsh.'

She turned around, tilting her head from left to right as she considered it.

'If you add some colour it would make things seem more homely, too. A painting here…some cushions. Maybe fresh flowers every now and then. I hear there are roses available at the estate.'

She was smiling as she turned back to him, but stopped when she saw his face.

'What?'

'I can't do any of that.'

'Right, of course. This isn't actually your house.'

'No,' he said mildly. 'Doesn't mean I can't be impressed at how easy this comes to you, though.'

'My job? Yeah, I would hope so.'

He shook his head. 'You're good at seeing solutions.'

Seeing solutions?

She *was* good at that. She did it for her siblings. Helping Hattie raise Georgie…helping Rob with his learning disability. She stepped in when her parents needed help with the house, or with a dinner party they were throwing, or anything they called on her for. She was doing it now with her grandmother's wedding. With the estate. Hell, with the entire island.

She'd always known that she was good at stepping in when she was needed, but for the first time she saw how that had translated to her professional life. Her entire business was solution-orientated. Someone didn't like their house? She would fix it! Someone needed to transform a property so it could be rented? She could do that! Someone needed help figuring out who to market their property to? She knew what to do!

Her entire life was built around a skill that sometimes she wished she didn't have.

No, that wasn't true. She enjoyed her job. She liked helping people. It was just that the expectation that she *would* help—at least in her personal life—made her feel…trapped.

It was the first time in her life she'd acknowledged it—and it made her hate herself.

'I've said the wrong thing.'

It was more an observation than a question. Elliott had been watching Morgan closely. He'd seen the way her lashes fluttered. The way her expression had drawn tight. The way she'd opened up to him and then, after his comment, snapped shut.

He hadn't meant to make the observation out loud either, and now he felt like a lumbering giant who'd been given a precious human artifact and was struggling not to crush it in his hands.

But Morgan only smiled. A fake smile that didn't reach her eyes and made him long for the earlier version of her. The one who had smiled easily, whose laughter had lit up her entire face. He had robbed her of that—robbed himself, too. But he understood it. It was more familiar to him than whatever had been unfolding between them before.

He used that knowledge to bolster himself. To soothe the ache he hadn't given permission to take root in his body.

'It has nothing to do with you,' she said. 'I just…'

She gave him a shaky smile. Again, so different from the ones she'd given him before.

'Come on, let's get you upstairs. I'll give you permission to boss me around once we get you settled in bed.'

In other circumstances he would have enjoyed this. Hell, a mere hour ago he'd thought he'd have the opportunity to get her to a bedroom. It wasn't even in the realm of possibility now.

She dealt with him almost clinically.

She decided, once she had him seated on the bed, that he'd feel better after a bath. So she ran him one, then helped him to the bathroom, telling him firmly that he could take it from there.

He did as he was told, and the minute he sank

into the warm water he sighed in gratitude. The knots in his body eased, and the aches he'd felt subsided to a dull throb. When he was done, he tied a towel around his waist, testing his weight on his ankle. It still hurt. It would probably take anti-inflammatories and ice to get it to a manageable level of pain.

He'd told Morgan where they were, and since he heard sounds coming from his bedroom he figured she was already there, sorting everything out.

He limped out through the door. Morgan had obviously heard him coming and turned.

'Right, so I've got your pills—'

She stopped. Stared.

It was a completely disarming stare. Her lips were parted, her eyes wide. And in them he was able to see a mixture of surprise and…desire. Lust, really. Hot and wild and completely unencumbered by whatever had caused her to withdraw before.

He had never been a vain person, but he couldn't help the way his posture changed. His chest puffed out, his shoulders pulled back, and his spine straightened. The hours he spent in the gym, trying to relieve the stress of his workdays, trying to forget the pain of the loneliness he refused to dwell on, were finally doing more than simply helping his mental and emotional health.

He was tempting this woman.

His woman.

His woman?

Where the hell had that come from?

But it didn't matter when she was looking at him like that. When she was walking towards him. He didn't move, didn't even breathe, too scared he might do something to mess things up again.

She stopped steps away from him. 'You're doing this on purpose,' she said.

'What?'

'Tempting me.'

'Tempting?'

'Oh, don't look so smug,' she said crossly. 'You're well aware—'

And then she stopped, her eyes dipping down. At the same moment he felt cool air over his body. His *entire* body.

His towel had come loose.

He swore silently—because, contrary to what she believed, he didn't want to seduce her. Well, he did, but not like this. He didn't want to worry about what was going on in her head when he kissed her, teased her, claimed her.

He quickly bent to retrieve the towel before his body betrayed his imagination. When he looked back at Morgan she was looking at the ceiling.

'Are you done?' she asked in a small voice.

Great. He'd embarrassed her.

'Yes. I'm sorry. It wasn't intentional.'

'Are you sure?' She quirked her brow. 'You came out of the bathroom wearing nothing but a towel and then it "magically" fell to the ground...'

There was a beat of silence.

'I didn't have any clothes.'

'That's what they all say,' she replied dryly. 'For the record, there are easier ways of showing me...that.'

Heat stirred in his body, but it quickly cooled when he saw that she'd covered her hand with her mouth.

'I didn't mean to say that,' she said, the sound muffled.

He only looked at her. Then, when her cheeks pinkened, he gave a quiet laugh.

Her gaze jumped to his, accusation bright. 'Are you *laughing* at me?'

'I wouldn't dare.'

She tilted her head, then stuck her tongue out before slipping her arm under his and helping him to the bed. He kept a hand firmly on his towel this time, not even letting go when he sat down.

'Let me get you some clothes. Please,' she added.

He resisted the urge to smile again as he told her where his clothes were, and she left him to get dressed. He did so slowly, trying to figure out why things were so confusing between them. It didn't help when she returned with a sandwich and a cup of tea.

'Eat,' she commanded. 'When you're done, take the pills.' She pointed to the glass of water and pills on his bedside cabinet. 'You don't have an ice pack in your fridge, so I put ice in a plastic bag and wrapped it in one of your dish cloths. It'll have to do for now. I'll get one on my way into town and bring it for you tomorrow. No point in coming back later, when you'll be fast asleep because of those pills.'

Confusion gave way to something stronger, though he could still feel it. The foundation of whatever wave of emotion had crashed over him.

She had driven him home, helped him inside. Run a bath for him, got his clothes ready. Made food for him, got him medication. She had taken care of him—*was* taking care of him—even though he'd said something to upset her earlier.

'Why are you doing this for me?' he asked.

She blinked. 'What do you mean? You hurt yourself.'

'I would have managed.'

'Why should you have to if I'm here?' she asked, brow furrowing.

'I've always managed.' He knew his reply was terse, but she was making all this seem small, when it wasn't.

Her eyes flickered. 'Yeah, well, sometimes you shouldn't have to. Especially on this island. You'll always have help here.'

CHAPTER ELEVEN

MORGAN SHOULD HAVE known once she told her grandmother about Elliott's fall that it wouldn't be a secret for long.

When she pulled in front of Elliott's house the next day her car was one of several. Dr Sam's car was right in front, followed by Sharon's. That meant all her grandmother's friends would be there, since Sharon was their designated driver.

Plus her grandmother herself.

Edna had insisted on coming with Morgan that morning.

This was all her fault. Elliott probably hated her.

She turned to Edna. 'Behave when you get inside, okay?'

'What does that mean?' Edna demanded. 'I always behave.'

Morgan looked at her.

Edna looked back.

After a while, Morgan sighed. 'Fine, you always behave. There definitely haven't been any times when you've said inappropriate things or intervened when you want things to go your way.'

Edna's jaw dropped. 'How long have you been keeping *that* inside?'

Morgan put a hand over her mouth and blushed. She hadn't meant to say that. It had rolled off her tongue without a thought.

'I'm sorry.' She dropped her hand. 'I don't know where that came from.'

'Keep it up,' Edna said after a moment, patting Morgan's thigh. 'If you do, you'll be able to tell your parents to step up in no time.'

With those words, Edna got out of the car.

Morgan stared after her, then hurried to follow. Her grandmother was in the house before Morgan could ask her what she meant, and then they were swarmed by people, all demanding the details of what had happened the previous day.

'Edna told us Elliott fell,' Joyce said, a hand on her chest. 'Was it because of the flowers? Did you push him?'

'I did not push—'

Clarice didn't give Morgan the chance to finish.

'Of course she didn't push him. She was quite happy about the flowers. Accepted them with open arms.'

Morgan glanced over and got a wink in return. Had Clarice seen what had happened the day before? There was no way. Morgan was absolutely sure there had been no one lurking in the shadows. Not to mention the fact that Clarice wouldn't have been able to resist helping if she'd seen Elliott fall. She hadn't been there. So she must be taking Morgan's side because she could tell Morgan was outnumbered.

Morgan accepted the help with a smile, and immediately diverted the conversation. She did not want to tell them the truth about Elliott's fall. She had been purposely vague when her grandmother had asked.

'Where is Elliott?' she asked. 'I thought you'd have asked *him* all these questions.'

'He's upstairs with Dr Sam,' Sharon said. 'He said he felt light-headed.'

Morgan pursed her lips. 'How long after you arrived did he say that?'

'Oh, not long. Maybe fifteen minutes?'

'Uh-huh.' Morgan forced herself not to laugh. 'How long ago was that?'

'Another fifteen minutes,' Joyce said. 'Dr Sam must be doing a thorough job of examining him. Either that, or the fall was more serious than either of you let on.'

'Hmm.' Morgan didn't think it was either of those options. 'I'd better go upstairs to check.'

'You do that, dear,' Edna said. 'I have some biscuits in the car,' she told her friends. 'I thought one of you might have been making him some food.'

'So did I!' Clarice said. 'I didn't make lasagne, because I thought Joyce would be making butter chicken and I didn't want to overwhelm him with food.'

'I did bring my butter chicken,' Joyce replied. 'But I also brought biscuits. I'm not an amateur.'

Morgan left them in the kitchen with a smile, before pressing the button for the elevator.

When the door opened Edna exclaimed, 'There's an *elevator*!' and the topic swiftly changed to the house.

Morgan was still smiling when she knocked on the bedroom door. There was a long wait before anyone answered, and then Dr Sam opened.

She was five or so years younger than Morgan's grandmother, her countenance kinder. She walked with the confidence of someone who knew what she was doing, and the grace of someone who didn't hold that knowledge over people's heads. She was one of seven doctors on the island, one of two GPs, and she breathed a sigh of relief when she saw who was at the door.

'It's only Morgan,' she called over her shoulder, then gave Morgan a smile. 'I'm so glad it's you. The others have been stressing my patient out. His blood pressure was much higher than I would have liked it to be.'

'You checked his blood pressure?'

'He was feeling light-headed.'

'I'm pretty sure he only said that because he

was trying to escape my grandmother's friends,' Morgan said as she walked into the room.

Elliott didn't say a word, only watched her from the bed. He was wearing track pants and a T-shirt, and somehow still managed to look put together. Come to think of it, the only time he hadn't looked put together had been the day before, when he'd come out of the bathroom.

She really didn't want to remember him coming out of the bathroom. She didn't want to think about how wondrous he'd looked. His shoulders, chest, biceps...all gleaming with the faintest hint of water. His body had looked as if it had been crafted with the sole intention of making her fall to her knees.

She had thought that the day before, too, and it had been as alarming then. And that had been *before* his towel had dropped and she'd caught a glimpse of his—

No.

She refused to think about that again, or to rehash the dirty thoughts that came with it. She was just going to make sure he was okay. Then she was going to work—and *keep* working—so the image of his glorious body, and one part in particular, faded from her mind.

'It's higher than I'd like, so I'd suggest keeping him calm,' Dr Sam said, unaffected by the tension crackling in the room. 'I'll be back later to check it again—if that's okay, Elliott?'

Elliott grunted.

'I'll take that as a yes,' Dr Sam said with a smile. 'You'll have to excuse me now. I have other patients. But, Elliott, please take the pain medication when you need it. And call me if things get worse.'

'Thank you,' Elliott said.

She nodded, then gave Morgan a kind smile before leaving the room.

The tension turned up a notch. Before it overtook them, Morgan spoke. 'Is…everything okay?' She tilted her head towards the door Dr Sam had left by. 'You're going to live?'

'Yes.' He waited a beat. 'It's a mild sprain. It'll heal within two weeks, and the other aches and pains will fade sooner. I have medication. I need to elevate the ankle and keep it iced.'

'That's good news. About it being mild.' She cleared her throat. 'I…um… I brought you an ice pack.'

'Thank you.' He studied her. 'I need to stay off my leg for at least a week.'

'I figured.'

'The timing is inconvenient.'

'There's never a convenient time to sprain your ankle,' she pointed out.

'I meant—'

'I know what you meant,' she interrupted. 'You're worried about the project without your presence. But it'll be fine.'

Briskly, she outlined what would be done in the next week, all the things that would continue without his physical presence.

'You're taking a lot on your shoulders,' he commented when she was done.

'That was always going to be the case, your sprained ankle or not.' She shrugged. 'I'll keep you updated at every step. We can do daily check-ins. I'll even show you our progress via video chat, if you like.'

'I'd appreciate that.'

He spoke gruffly. Something was clearly bothering him. She waited, but he didn't elaborate.

'What about the wedding?' he asked eventually.

'What about it?'

'Won't this affect your work on that?'

'My work for the wedding is to make sure the wedding venue is ready. Which basically means that I'm already doing it by doing the work on the estate.' She tilted her head. 'Is that what you're worried about? That all this is keeping me too busy to help with the wedding?'

'I don't want you to make sacrifices for me.'

She thought about what he'd asked her the day before. *Why are you doing this for me?* What he said now was an echo of that—which, in turn, was an echo of something else.

It must have something to do with his family. Based on what he'd told her about them, he didn't know how to handle it when people cared about him. Or rather, when people *showed* him they cared about him. So now he was bracing himself for her to hurt him in some way because he thought he was making things difficult for her.

She didn't know how to tell him that that ship had sailed a long time ago. From the moment Grandma Edna had called Elliott had been making things difficult for Morgan. Things had only gone downhill from there. She was fixing up an entire estate, for heaven's sake, hoping to boost the economy of the island while she was at it. 'Difficult' was the minimum of how she'd describe what was happening.

And still she stayed.

Maybe she shouldn't.

Maybe she was giving him false hope by staying.

By doing that was she telling him that she'd always be around, even when he treated her poorly? Not that he *was* treating her poorly. It was just… that was how things had started with her family. Her constant support had become the reason they constantly expected it—and never appreciated it.

Was she teaching Elliott to treat her the same way? And would that eventually lead to the hurt he was expecting? From her? *For* her?

'I'm not making any sacrifices for you,' she said now, a little primly. She was trying to keep the tangle of emotions out of her voice. 'I have things managed at the estate, which means I have them managed for the wedding. My part in it, anyway. The rest of the wedding is being handled by the four women downstairs—who, for the record, have already planned each of your meals, including teatime treats, for at least the next three days. They'll probably rejoice when they hear they might be getting to help you for weeks.'

He winced.

'They'll behave,' she told him. 'My grandmother promised.'

'You believe that?'

Her lips curved. 'No. But what can you do? Now, while I have you, I've had an email from…'

Purposefully, she delved into business. There wasn't really anything urgent she needed to discuss with him, and he seemed to know it. His gaze flickered to hers, narrowing, but it went back to normal seconds later and she pretended she hadn't seen it. Slowly the tension eased from his face.

Relief unspooled in her stomach, but seconds later a sinister kind of tightness curled around her heart and squeezed.

Somehow in all of this she had taken responsibility for Elliott's emotions. For making him feel better. She didn't know how that made *her* feel. Especially since she was now dealing with the realisation that she was unhappy with the way things were with her family.

Surely she needed to work through that before she opened herself to a new relationship? Did she even *want* a relationship? Was that what Elliott wanted?

There were too many questions, too many layers to whatever was happening between her and Elliott. This was why she didn't examine her feelings. She'd rather keep busy, not work through anything, and be just fine with her life.

Maybe she should put some distance between her and Elliott.

'I should probably go,' Morgan said after a short bit of silence. 'Can't slack off with the boss out.'

'I'm not your boss.'

'Aren't you?' she asked casually, though really it was a serious question that didn't only refer to work.

His brow knitted, but he didn't comment.

'You'll be okay?' she asked. He nodded. 'Do you want me to come over later?'

That's not distance, Morgan.

Elliott shifted before she could examine that thought. Something about the movement bothered her. It wasn't that he was in pain—she'd seen him deal with that, and it wasn't like this. But she couldn't ask him about it without veering into territory she'd already breached by asking him if he wanted her to visit later.

'No,' he said finally. 'You don't have to come.'

I want to.

The words almost left her lips, but she snatched them back, telling herself to take the win. But as she dragged herself to the door it didn't feel like a win. She looked over her shoulder, saw Elliott leaning back against the pillows, eyes closed, his posture more defeated than she'd ever seen on him.

Although everything inside her told her to go back, to shake it out of him, she walked out. Went to her car. Drove back to the estate. Started to work. Refused to think about him. And failed.

CHAPTER TWELVE

THIS LAST WEEK of Elliott's life had been unlike any other.

He'd had more people in his house than he actually knew on the island. Someone had always been popping in to check on him, bringing some form of food or entertainment. The fridge and freezer were packed with enough meals for, he suspected, the next century, and his living room now held a number of magazines and board games he'd never heard of.

The more he'd told people he could read or play games on his tablet, the more they'd waved off his suggestions. He'd stopped trying to tell them he had enough food, too. That had come after he'd said it to Sharon and she had laughed out loud and said, 'You never have enough food on Penguin Island.'

She'd promptly dished him up another plate of her admittedly brilliant chicken *alfredo* and told him to eat.

After day two of this invasion, he'd told himself to accept it. Nothing he said was going to change what the people of Penguin Island were doing for him. And once that resistance had gone away, he had finally been able to examine his emotions about it all. He supposed one of them was bemusement. Why were all these people being nice to him? They barely knew him. He was an outsider; he didn't deserve their kindness.

It made him think of how Morgan had helped him in those first few days. He hadn't deserved her kindness either, but she'd given it to him. Things had changed since then. Now when she called him, she did the bare minimum of checking in before immediately shifting to business. The project seemed to be going well, and he clung to that. The sooner it was done, the sooner he could leave the island and pretend the last confusing month had never happened.

Still, every day he missed Morgan. More than he had any right to. He'd told her not to visit—because he'd seen on her face that she didn't want to—and yet every day he wished she would.

It happened on the Sunday.

Edna knocked on his door, bright and early. This wasn't unusual; she'd been bringing him brownies every day since she'd discovered he liked them. It had bothered him at first—he had come here and threatened her wedding. But she seemed to have put that aside, probably because he had built the entire estate project around the event, and now she was dedicated to taking care of him. After he'd thought about that it had still bothered him, but somehow...less.

That morning though, Edna looked fierce as she entered his house. She usually knocked before letting herself in. Crime here was nearly non-existent, which was only one reason he left the door unlocked. It was the easier option. Otherwise he'd be walking to the door every hour at least, and that would prolong his recovery even more.

'My granddaughter has something to say to you.'

Elliott put down the cup of coffee he'd been drinking. He shifted, for the first time seeing an exasperated Morgan behind her grandmother. He folded his arms and leaned back on the couch.

Morgan quirked a brow at him. *Really?* it said. *You're encouraging this?*

He wanted to say he was unaffected by it, but he wasn't. His body immediately reacted to that eyebrow. The hair on his skin prickled, his blood heated, and he had to look at Edna to try and get other body parts under control.

He thought he'd stopped wanting people who didn't want him.

He breathed in at that, but Morgan was speaking, saving him from exploring it further.

'Elliott, I am sorry for not coming to see you this week,' she said, in a tone that sounded as if she was reciting the words. 'I should have abandoned all the work we need to get done so my grandmother's wedding can continue and offered you my company instead, reassured your ankle that it's doing an excellent job at healing.'

But it clearly wasn't a correct recital, because Edna poked Morgan in the stomach.

'Ow!' Morgan exclaimed. 'Why did you do that? You said I had to apologise, and I did.'

'That was not an apology,' Edna scolded. 'The man has sat here pining for you for a week and all you can offer him is sarcasm?'

'I wasn't pining,' Elliott interjected with a frown.

'Of course you were, dear.' Edna waved a hand. 'It was obvious to everyone who came here this week. We all thought Morgan would come to her senses, since she's been pining, too, but no. Apparently the two of you need me to intervene.'

'I was *not* pining,' Morgan said now. 'And even if I were—which I was *not*,' she assured Elliott, 'it isn't your place to intervene, Gran. I thought we'd gone over this?'

'Ha!' Edna exclaimed. 'We've not been over it. You let it slip and then apologised. But now that you've said it again, I'm forced to believe it and act on it.' She bowed her head in mock humility. 'I shouldn't have forced you to come here, Morgan. Please accept my apology.'

With that, she walked out through the front

door. There was no mistaking the turning of the key in the lock.

Morgan looked at him. 'You gave her a key?'

'I did not,' he replied grimly.

Silence followed as they both stared at the door. Eventually Morgan walked to the kitchen. She looked striking in the black and white monochrome. She wore a bright red dress with hundreds of little flowers on it. The dress was scooped at her neckline, revealing the faintest of cleavage, and fell to her knees. Her hair was tied back with a white ribbon, a bow at the top of her ponytail, and her sandals had white straps with a sparkling circle between her two front toes.

He couldn't believe he was studying her in such detail that he had noticed the sparkling circles between her toes.

No, that was a lie. He could believe it. He wanted to know every detail about her. And as she stood in the kitchen, making his world brighter with her red dress, he wondered if it was a metaphor of some kind.

Was she there to change his world? To add colour to something he had, for the longest time, believed to be dull and bland? Or was this a warning? A sign to slow down or a sign of danger? A warning about what she would do to him?

'I hope you don't mind if I help myself to some coffee,' Morgan said, interrupting his annoying thoughts. 'It's been a pretty eventful morning, as you can imagine.'

'I can.'

'Can you?' She cast the question over her shoulder. 'Edna woke me up at six this morning—the one day I'd actually managed to sleep to six, mind you—and demanded I tell her why I've been avoiding you. She did not take me pulling the blankets over my head as an answer. In fact, she pulled the blankets *off* me, and demanded to know, once again, why I've been avoiding you.'

He didn't know what to say for the longest time. Then, 'There's cake. Brownies. Biscuits. Help yourself.'

'It's eight a.m.'

'You've been up since six, arguing with your grandmother. That makes it equivalent to at least noon.'

She gave a small laugh. 'You know what? I actually haven't eaten this morning, so I'm going to take you up on that offer.' She walked to his fridge. 'Have you? Eaten, I mean?'

'Yes.' Idly, he laid a hand on his stomach. 'That's all I do these days.'

'Are you implying that you look different from when I last saw you?' Her eyes skipped over him. 'I assure you, your stomach is still as it once was.'

It wasn't, and he was fine with it. But it was immensely pleasing that Morgan had looked at him in that way.

He tried to shake it off. His entire adult life people had looked at him *in that way*. He shouldn't be preening because Morgan was.

He shouldn't be, but he was.

Because Morgan was different.

'Can I at least get you another cup of coffee? A brownie?' she asked.

'If you must.'

'I'm not asking you to sacrifice your life,' she said with another laugh.

'I've already resigned myself to a slower recovery because of all the sugar I've consumed.'

'Generally, I find sugar *aids* recovery,' she offered helpfully. 'Are you…?' She cleared her throat. 'Are you feeling better?'

He nodded. 'Dr Sam is happy. She thinks I could be back on the ankle by Wednesday.'

'That's great.' She sounded relieved.

'Anything new at the estate?' he asked, as her relief tightened something inside him.

There wasn't, but still she talked him through their progress. She showed him pictures, videos, asked him for confirmation on a number of issues. She told him about how Edna's soon-to-be stepson had agreed to post the video on his social media and seemed fine with their plan to use his fame to lift the status of the island.

'I'm sure his father had something to do with that,' Morgan added, 'but we won't question the ways of the gods. Also, Thad has got a group of volunteers together. I mentioned the arch idea to him and he kind of jumped on it. So now they're building one for the garden. It might also turn into an altar of some kind… He cleared it with my grandmother, so honestly I didn't ask too many questions.'

'Thad?'

'Yeah,' she said with a faint smirk. 'You were right about him feeling bad, I think. So now he's being overly enthusiastic about how he can help.'

'He's been around the estate a lot?'

'Popped in once or twice.' She brought him a fresh cup of coffee and the brownie she'd heated, before settling at the kitchen table with a plate of food herself. 'Mostly to check in on the islanders. For their morale, I suppose.'

'How has that been?' he asked slowly. 'For you?'

She pierced a piece of pasta rather forcefully. 'Fine. He's been perfectly respectful.'

'He usually isn't?'

'No, it's not that. I just…usually avoid him.' She ate for a bit. 'And he avoids me, too. It's been awkward between us since…' She exhaled. 'Since we broke up. You saw.'

'Yes.' And because he couldn't help himself, he said, 'Tell me.'

She lifted her head, looking at him. Indecision creased her face, pursed her lips. Her eyes searched his, seeing things he probably didn't want her to. Then her expression softened, and he felt something akin to a key unlocking in his chest. Warmth rushed out, as if it had been locked behind that door, the pressure building, until finally it had been let out.

'I think I loved him,' she said before he could process what was happening to him. 'I was young and... I was tired.' She exhaled. 'There was a lot going on at home at that time. My sister was pregnant at seventeen, scared and still so innocent, even though she'd made a decision that would change her entire life. My brother had just been diagnosed with his learning disability and he was angry, like only a teenager can be. I'd been spreading myself thin, trying to manage it all while working on my degree, and my parents...' She shook her head. 'Anyway, I was feeling particularly vulnerable when I came to the island that year, and Thad was Thad. Charming, sincere, handsome. He made me the centre of his world and it was the most romantic thing.'

She pushed around the leftover pasta on her plate, before very deliberately eating a few bites. When she'd finished chewing them, she continued.

'It wasn't a healthy relationship. We were hiding it, for one thing, because we—no, because *I* didn't want anyone to know. And we didn't talk about anything real. It was all fluff and giddiness. And...and physical stuff,' she said in a shaky voice. 'I'm sorry. I don't know why that was so hard for me to say. I'm an adult. It's stupid.'

'Not stupid,' he growled.

The sides of her mouth quirked up. 'No, probably not.' She lifted a shoulder, dropped it. 'I hadn't had a physical relationship before him. He was my first kiss...my first touch.' Her cheeks pinkened. 'You get the point.'

He grunted now, because he did get the point, and he was insanely jealous that Thad had got to share something so precious with her.

'One night, we...um...got to a point when...' She cringed. 'No, you know what? This is stupid. I'm just going to say it. We almost had sex, but I chickened out. I was terrified of getting pregnant. I didn't trust that the condom wouldn't break. I wasn't on hormonal contraception, and I wasn't going to destroy my life or a child's life because—' She broke off on a gasp. 'That's awful. Oh, no...' she moaned. 'That's an awful thing to say.'

Elliott had no idea what to do. He'd never been in this position before, where someone had shared something so intimate with him. And it clearly was intimate. Even from where he sat, he could see the faint trembling of Morgan's body.

He wanted to go over, pull her into his arms. He didn't know if he should. If he *could*. Would he be crossing a line if he did? Was it the right thing to do? He'd failed too many times, his instincts letting him down. He didn't want to do the wrong thing now and make Morgan feel worse.

But something stronger than instinct urged him up. He made his way to her slowly, so she'd see him coming—and also because he had no choice with his leg—and stopped right at her side. She tipped her head to look up at him, her eyes open and vulnerable and looking for reassurance. And so he did what he wanted to do. He opened his arms, put them around her, and brought her close to his body.

The height of the kitchen chair elevated her so that she fitted snug against his chest. She relaxed into him. Made a cute little sound that might have been a sob. He was too terrified to check. Everything about this moment felt precarious. What if he shifted and things collapsed? What if she pushed him away…told him that this wasn't what she wanted? That *he* wasn't what she wanted?

For half his life he'd been made to feel that way—and it had broken him. He could finally admit that now, with Morgan in his arms, and that terrified him, too.

'I'm sorry,' she said after a bit, lifting her head. 'I shouldn't be so emotional.'

'Don't apologise,' he replied. 'I'm honoured that you would share that with me.'

She smiled, but bit her lip. It was probably inappropriate to find that sexy, but he did.

'Thank you,' she said.

'You're welcome.'

'Do you want me to help you back to your seat?'

'No.'

His heart was beating faster, speeding up the natural rhythm of his breathing. He knew it was because of her, because of her smile, and because of the softness she was staring at him with.

He sat down next to her, not wanting to take a chance. But she was eating again, and he didn't think it was because she was hungry. Was he making her nervous? Should he have gone back to the couch? Given her space?

'The day that happened,' Morgan said suddenly, pushing her now empty plate aside, 'my sister went into labour.'

She turned to face him, her elbow sliding onto the counter. She rested her head in her hand.

'She tried to call me but I'd turned my phone off. I'd wanted to be…free. To pretend I didn't have all those responsibilities. And I… I missed my niece's birth.'

'Why are you blaming yourself?' he asked, searching her face.

'Who else should I blame?'

'Blame implies wrongdoing. You did nothing wrong.'

'I *ignored* my sister's call.'

'She made it to the hospital?' he asked.

She nodded.

'Your niece is healthy?'

Another nod.

'And you adore her.'

A soft smile curved her face. 'Without question.'

'Which is why I didn't pose it as one,' he said dryly.

She snorted.

'Everything turned out fine, Morgan. It makes no sense for you to feel guilty.'

Morgan became so still a feeling of alarm went through Elliott. But he could see her chest rising and falling quietly, as if she'd decided her breathing was bothering him.

'Feelings make no sense,' she pointed out eventually. 'It's been eight years, and I still feel the embarrassment of breaking up with Thad because I was scared of what would happen if I stayed with him. And the guilt of missing Georgie's birth will always be there.'

He frowned. 'You're punishing yourself.'

Now she stiffened. 'I am not.'

'Okay…'

'Don't just say "okay" because you don't want to argue.'

'Okay.'

She shook her head. 'You're infuriating.'

'Yes,' he acknowledged. 'But so are you.'

'*Me*? What did I do?'

'You can't see that your break-up with Thad was inevitable. If the physical side of your relationship was the only thing keeping you together it would have ended anyway.' He continued before she could object. 'As for the situation with your sister—you are not her parent. You aren't responsible for her.'

She was shaking her head before he finished. 'You don't understand—'

'I understand complicated family dynamics.'

'Not mine. I don't have a personal life, Elliott. None. No friends, no steady relationship since Thad. I go to work, I go home, and I wait. I wait for my family to need me.'

She put a hand on the counter. Not quite a slam, but close enough.

'I bought a house that needs work because it gives me something to do, but it's not something so consuming I won't be there for them.'

His heart cracked. Warmth oozed from it. Sympathy, frustration, anger—and more. Something deeper. He didn't examine it since she wasn't finished.

'And my job...' She squeezed her eyes shut and took a deep breath. 'I've had several people approach me with projects that would take me out of Cape Town...'

'You turned them down?'

She nodded. 'I was afraid I wouldn't be there when they needed me.'

Punishing yourself for not being there once. He didn't get a chance to say it.

'I've sacrificed so much for them.'

'Why?' he asked.

She blinked. 'What do you mean, why? They're my family.' Then her lashes fluttered as her gaze came to rest on him. 'Maybe you *do* understand that. Otherwise, why would you be here on the island at all?'

CHAPTER THIRTEEN

IT MIGHT HAVE been a little sneaky, but Morgan was worried she'd shared too much. Her emotions were finally freeing themselves from the hole she'd dug for them—for *Elliott*. It felt as if they'd been waiting for this moment all week. It must be part of the reason she'd been struggling to sleep.

Every night she would tumble into bed, exhausted, but her brain would go through everything she needed to do the next day. Over and over and over again. Until she looked at her clock and saw it was some early-morning hour. The anxiety of not sleeping would keep her up for another hour, then she would eventually fall into a restless sleep minutes before her alarm went off.

And everything would start all over again.

She hadn't been able to pinpoint the exact cause of her insomnia. Of course she was juggling multiple things at once, with higher stakes than any of her other projects, so it made sense for her to be struggling. But she'd also been fighting the urge to visit Elliott. Probably because she'd known the minute she saw him she'd tell him her every secret.

And now things had shifted in their relationship. She could feel their new intimacy in her soul, upsetting her equilibrium. The only way she knew how to handle it was to coax his secrets out, too.

It was sneaky, as she'd thought, and she wasn't proud of it.

'I know what you're doing,' Elliott said.

'I have no doubt that you do.' She sighed. 'Come on, let's go sit on the couch. You can't be comfortable like this.'

He didn't say anything as he hop-shuffled back to the couch, with her hovering at his side, ready to jump in if he asked for help. He didn't, and they both sat down. Their bodies were close together, but it was too late for Morgan to shift without drawing attention to the movement.

And still he wasn't saying anything.

She began to regret that she'd pried—or tried to, at least, since prying would mean that she'd actually asked a question. She hadn't. She'd made an implication about his family, but that was it. She'd wanted to shift the focus, hoping to make herself feel better, and now it was—

Her thoughts stopped when she felt an unfamiliar warmth at her hand. She looked down, staring blankly at their entwined fingers. And then she paid attention to her body. There'd been a spinning in her chest that had stilled once he'd made contact. Now that spinning was in her stomach. A soft tightening and releasing. Not uncomfortable, but alarming.

'I've wanted to do this since I came into the kitchen,' he said softly. 'I've been thinking about it since then, too. Going back and forth about whether it's the right thing.'

She couldn't stop staring at their hands. More at his than hers, caught by the swells of his knuckles, the dusting of hair, the strength that seemed impossible to tell from a hand and yet was somehow there.

'I don't think you've done a single thing that hasn't been right since I came to this house,' she replied. 'Except maybe siding with my grandmother this morning.'

'I got this, didn't I?' he asked, squeezing her hand.

She laughed. 'Touché.' A beat later, she asked, 'Why would you doubt your instincts?'

He didn't answer; she didn't push. Not when his face looked the way it did. Raw. Honest. Had she thought his expressions unreadable before? Muted? She was a fool. Or perhaps merely uneducated in the enigma that was Elliott.

She wanted to change that.

She hadn't planned on acting on that thought,

but before she knew it her free hand was cupping his face.

Their eyes held. And then he turned and kissed the palm of her hand.

It stole her breath, that simple contact. It felt more intense than the kiss they'd shared at the beach. Even when he'd carried her to the house it hadn't felt like this.

'My instincts have led me astray,' he admitted quietly. 'With my family. My parents, specifically. They always seemed to care more about my brother than me. Everything Gio did was more important. I tried…' He pulled away from her, letting go of her hands, and rubbed a hand over his jaw. 'I followed my instincts, trying to get them to notice me. Excelled at sport. Worked hard at school. Nothing I did could measure up to my genius brother.'

'I'm so sorry.'

He shook his head. 'It's fine.'

'No, Elliott,' she said with a shake of her head. 'It's not fine. Not when they made you feel…' She trailed off, unsure whether he wanted her to say it.

'That was why I was so confused when you took care of me,' he said roughly. 'I'd done nothing to deserve your kindness.'

Her heart broke for him. For the young boy who'd thought his actions would dictate how his parents treated him. Who, because those actions had never been enough, didn't think *he* was enough.

'You don't have to do anything to deserve kindness, Elliott. Although in this case you have.'

His eyebrows lifted.

'You're the reason my grandmother can have her wedding here. You've employed a good number of people on the island. You've even come up with a way to help the island succeed after your departure.'

'That last thing was you.'

'Us,' she insisted. 'I wouldn't have come up with the idea if it hadn't been for you.'

He didn't reply to that, but the silence that spread between them was easy. They didn't touch one another again, and she was happy with that. It gave her a chance to settle. This morning had been a lot. She was desperate for...

She wasn't quite sure. Sanity? Stability?

'There have been so many people in my house,' he grumbled.

And then it hit her. She was desperate for levity.

'Oh, man, that must have freaked you out.'

'They touched my things,' he said in a low voice. 'Opened my fridge. *Talked* to me.'

She pursed her lips, but the laugh slipped out anyway. Once she'd started, she couldn't stop. His face was priceless. He was *disgusted* that people had talked to him. People he barely knew...who barely knew him. These people had come into his house, touched his things, opened his fridge, and *talked* to him.

Maybe disgusted wasn't the right word. Confused was probably more accurate. But it didn't matter. Not when she was already laughing harder, apologising in huffs of breath.

After a second his lips twitched. His eyes crinkled. And then he was laughing, too. The tension in her shoulders was released, the knot in her belly eased and, strangely, a wave of sleepiness washed over her. But she resisted it, enjoying her freedom instead. Finally, they stopped, but lightness was still in the air.

'It's been an experience,' he muttered, with a twist of his mouth.

'I can imagine.'

'Will it keep happening after I get back on my feet?'

'Yes. I'm sorry, but it's true! This community is…' She threw her hands up. 'They care about people. And now that you're part of it—'

'I am *not* part of this community.'

The dark way he said it sucked some of the lightness out of the air.

'They'll always see you as part of the community now. You're giving them jobs. Potentially saving the island they love.' She shrugged, no longer able to resist the tiredness. 'Plus, you're a good person, Elliott.'

Letting her tired brain take over, she curled onto her side, resting her head on his lap. He froze, but then slowly began to stroke her hair.

'You say nice things because…' He hesitated. 'Because you care about me?'

'Yeah,' she answered, stifling a yawn. 'But that doesn't mean I'm wrong.'

She fell asleep before she could hear his reply.

CHAPTER FOURTEEN

ON ELLIOTT'S FIRST full day back, Morgan handed him a clipboard with a long list of everything that would now be his responsibility.

'We're in it now,' she said with dark amusement, and proceeded to inform him that all the rental houses in Flipper Estate had been booked by wedding guests.

Most of the structural work on the estate had been completed, though there was still some way to go on some of the houses that had more damage than the others. They'd be cutting it close in fixing those by the wedding, but Morgan was confident they could do it. The estate aesthetic was coming together, with all the renovated houses painted a pretty blue and white. And the garden was, without a doubt, the most magnificent thing he'd seen.

It was a medium-sized open space, not unlike the gardens back home in Cape Town, enclosed by a silver fence partially obscured by trees. His attention was immediately drawn to the big oak tree on his left as he entered the garden. Its thick crooked branches exploded in leaves, casting shadows over a significant portion of the garden. Flowers sprang up all over—red, yellow, white— bringing colour to an otherwise sea of green.

He hadn't visited the garden until now. Technically, it wasn't a part of the renovation, so he hadn't seen the need. That had seemed particularly true when he'd thought it more likely he'd bump into Edna or any one of her friends there, since it was the wedding venue.

Elliott was aware of the shift that had brought him to the garden today, but he wasn't interested in doing any more than acknowledging it. What had happened between him and Morgan the previous week had been... Well, it *had* been. No point in thinking about it further.

Liar, an inner voice whispered.

Fine. He'd thought about it. About her trusting him enough to tell him about her family. About her fears. She'd even said she cared about him, and his heart had expanded to double its size. Which meant he was finally feeling full again, after his family's rejection had halved his heart in the first place.

Perhaps it wasn't that he didn't want to examine it, but rather that he had no idea what to do now that he had.

'You don't like it?' Morgan asked from beside him.

Slowly, he turned. 'I do.'

'So why are you frowning?'

He looked back at the garden, eager to shift the blame to something other than his emotions. Conveniently, his eyes rested on Thad. The mayor was working with a group of about five people on a wooden altar. Not far away, another group was constructing an arch of some kind. Elliott had seen them on his initial scan of the garden, but he hadn't realised Thad was there.

'What did you tell him when you broke up with him?' he asked quietly.

If she was surprised by the question, she didn't show it. 'That I wasn't ready for a relationship. And I certainly wasn't ready for what we were about to do.' She moved in front of him. 'Are you planning on defending my honour?'

'Do you want me to?'

She tilted her head, eyes twinkling. 'I kind of do, yeah.'

Then with a small smile—and a resulting leap of his heart—she shook her head.

'Come on, we have more important things to do than talk about my ex.'

She stalked past him and he followed with a smile of his own, before being thrown into the deep end with work.

The next two weeks passed in a blur. They worked day and night on the estate, where everyone was putting in more than their fair share of effort to try and get it done on time.

Whenever Elliott could spare a moment, he checked in on his own business. He attended virtual meetings while walking from one house to another; answered client phone calls in the middle of painting a room; soothed employee tensions at the warehouse as he helped carry furniture into houses.

Things were busier than they had ever been for him, and he didn't mind it a single bit. Because in between all the craziness was Morgan.

They shared looks when something ridiculous happened. Talked about it as they walked into town to get lunch. They joked about the work, and about the wedding, because laughter was the only way to manage the pressure.

Sometimes late at night, when the last of the workers had finally left, they shared a beer on the porch of one of the houses. Those nights were his favourite, because she'd talk about her work then. About projects she'd done, or projects she would do once the wedding was over. He loved to watch her as she talked. As she *sparkled*. Because this was her passion.

She'd turn to him without fail and ask him about his own work, and he'd tell her. Share with her things he never had before.

'You're proud of what you've done,' she remarked one night, smiling at him. 'As well you should be.'

'I… I am,' he replied, surprised that he could admit it. Surprised that he hadn't admitted it, even to himself, before.

These surprises were becoming more frequent with the more time he spent with Morgan. She complimented him so easily, pointed out things he did well. She also pointed out things he didn't do well, but it never sounded condescending. Never as if she was comparing him to anyone else.

Whenever he had those thoughts, he realised how much his youth still affected him. Some part of him had been indoctrinated never to acknowledge his successes, to keep on pushing because they were never enough.

He'd been giving his brother only the vaguest of updates, and whenever Gio prodded, Elliott wouldn't reply. Because deep down he was afraid he'd made a mistake by going in this direction with the estate. What if things didn't work out the way he intended? Should he have just done what Gio had asked him to do? Gio was, after all, a genius.

But then Morgan would say something nice to him, or her excitement about the progress on the estate or the wedding would spill over onto him, and he'd feel better. He had no idea what to do about it. He'd never had a relationship like this.

Where there was more than superficial commonality or physical attraction.

Although the physical attraction was certainly there. He thought about it all the time, in fact. And worried that acting on it would spoil whatever they were building.

'Are you ever going to tell me why you're doing this?' Morgan asked one night, a week before the wedding. It was Friday, everyone had gone home, and they were sitting on the porch of the house they'd just finished. 'We've talked about all kinds of things, but you haven't said a word about that.'

He swirled the contents of his bottle, looking up into the night sky. If he sat perfectly still he could hear the crash of the ocean. With Morgan at his side, he felt…content.

Content? Not once in his life had he ever used that as a description for himself. There was always more. Always ways to expand his business. Always another person to charm—which was a very loose way to think about what he'd done with women in the past. The point was that 'more' had become his way of life.

But that happens when you don't think you're enough.

He took a swig of the beer, swallowing it down along with the emotion that thought awakened. 'My father had a heart attack.'

Her head whipped to the side. 'What? Is he okay?'

'He's fine. It could have been worse.'

He stilled. How would he have felt if his mother had called to tell him the heart attack *had* been worse? He couldn't answer. Hell, he barely knew how he felt about it now.

'The doctor wants him to rest, which means no work.'

'So you stepped in?'

'My brother called to ask me if I would.' His fingernail worried the label of the beer bottle. 'He never asks for anything. I… I couldn't say no.'

'Because you're a big ol' softy beneath that hard exterior,' she teased, but quickly sobered. 'And because families are complicated and you didn't know how to say no.'

He was constantly amazed at how well she knew him. Constantly annoyed, too. He muttered a curse.

She gave a soft laugh. 'What was that for?'

'You.'

'You *swore* at me?'

'Not specifically.' His exhalation made him sound like a bull. 'You see things other people don't.'

'Oh, yes, that clarifies the swearing thing,' she said wryly. 'Go right ahead and defile this new house with your dirty words.'

Slowly, he turned his head. 'You're worried about the house's innocence?'

Her gaze met his. 'My own, actually.'

She could have said *Take off your clothes* and it wouldn't have heated him as much as those words did. Or was it because of the way she was looking at him? Because of the lazy desire in her eyes, as if she was turned on but couldn't be bothered by it?

He could change that. He could bother her if she let him.

He didn't even care that these thoughts were dangerous—the kind he avoided whenever he was around her. The kind he *fought* whenever he was around her. He'd come to accept that sexual tension would be their constant companion. That the cloud of lust following them would always be threatening to burst into a thunderstorm of seduction.

It was in the looks he caught her aiming at him when he was working. The way she sometimes tilted her head, bit her lip. The power of it triggered something primitive inside him. Made him want to pull off his shirt, beat his chest, roar.

The only way to make it abate was to touch her whenever he could. When she asked him to pass her something he grazed her fingers, eager to feel their softness. He touched the small of her back when she went through a door ahead of him. She never complained, touched him, too, and on those days he'd dream of her. Of touching her, licking her, doing wicked things to her. And then he'd wake up sweating and aroused, unable to sleep for the rest of the night.

'I only take innocence when it's offered,' he all but growled.

Morgan's brows rose. There was no judgement in her gaze, no reprimand. Only curiosity, amusement. *Fire.* 'Are you propositioning me?'

'That's not what "offered" means.'

'Hmm...'

She set down her beer and stood, turning to him. Nothing about the movement was hasty or alarming, yet his heartbeat sped up. His muscles tensed. It was a ridiculous reaction to someone hooking their thumbs around the straps of their denim dungarees. But he'd been staring at her in those dungarees for weeks. She wore them whenever she painted.

'It's an unspoken rule that if you're going to paint a house, this is what you wear,' she'd said when he had commented on it. 'It makes no sense, since it's not really comfortable, but I don't make the rules.'

But she altered them. Her dungarees were sometimes made of a flimsy material that clung to every curve and dimple of her body. She only wore a sports bra underneath, from what he could see. Probably underwear, too, though he never looked long enough to figure that out. He didn't want to get caught, for one thing. For another, he was afraid of what imagining her without underwear as she stood beside him every day would do to his brain.

His body.

'We've been avoiding this,' she said conversationally.

'Yes.'

'You sprained your ankle last time.'

He grunted.

'But that isn't why we've been avoiding it, is it?'

'No,' he replied, setting his own beer down. He stood now, too, but didn't walk any closer.

'It's a terrible idea,' she informed him, but took the tiniest step towards him. 'It will muddle things.'

He took a step forward. 'Yes.'

'We might not come out unscathed.'

'There's no "might",' he contradicted. 'We won't.'

The vulnerability on her face all but jumped at him. It slammed into his chest, his heart, and that traitorous organ told him it didn't want to come out unscathed. He was in love with her, and he wanted something to show for it. *Her* heart, he realised, but he shut that thought down, looking at her face again.

'Don't do anything you don't want to.'

'I...want to,' she said softly. 'With you.'

He'd asked her to offer—and she was. He knew what it cost her, too. She'd stopped things from progressing with Thad because she'd been afraid of what it might lead to. She hadn't dated much after him because she was afraid of the cost. She was sacrificing those fears for him. If he'd had any chance of resisting her before, he didn't now.

He closed the space between them. She was trembling when he did. His body demanded that he take her, take his fill. Show her just how much he could make her tremble now that he had the chance.

He wanted to touch every part of her body. To kiss her mouth, her breasts, lower. He wanted to lick, to taste, to feel her writhing beneath him.

But he knew that wasn't the way to go. He wanted to make this mean something. And while their passion, their insatiable thirst, would do that, too, he could tell that wasn't what she wanted.

He'd give her what she wanted.

It might kill him, but he would.

He lowered his head, taking his time as he studied her face, illuminated under the full moon. Her eyes held desire and trust, her lashes fluttering as he made her wait for the kiss. There was a blush on her cheeks. Her mouth was open, and warm breath heated his lips. He inhaled, felt that heat move to his heart, settle there in a way that had nothing to do with sensuality and spread.

With each heartbeat it reached further down his body. He ached for her. Chest, arms, torso. He was already aroused, had been from the moment she'd stood up, but when that heat hit between his legs he pulled her even closer, relishing her gasp.

He slid his hand over the small of her back, then cupped her butt, tilting his hips forward. Another gasp, this one inches from his lips because he'd moved closer. She gave a little moan—a protest, he thought, because he still wasn't kissing her.

But she would have to wait.

If he was going to torture them he would revel in it. Revel in the way her chest heaved against his, the press of her plush breasts, the tiniest pulse as she shifted her hips against his. The movement was so small—barely there—as if she didn't want him to notice she was trying to soothe the ache she must feel, too.

He smiled.

'Masochist,' she accused softly.

'Never before,' he said, adding a second hand to her butt. His body was screaming at him, unhappy with the restraint controlled by his mind, which his body had officially declared its enemy. 'It's you.'

'I'll bring you much more pain if you don't kiss me.'

'Kiss *me*,' he commanded.

The last thing he saw before her lips met his was her smile. Then he closed his eyes, sinking into the pleasure of finally, *finally* kissing her. Her mouth was warm and soft…familiar yet entirely unknown to him. A mountain or a forest he passed every day but never explored.

He explored now. He moved his tongue against hers in a battle they would both win. Took in every shiver that came with a certain angle, every moan when he changed the depth.

His hands moved, too, away from the curves they'd enjoyed until now, moving on to the rest of her body. He traced the arch of her back, his fingers lingering on her ribs before sliding up. His thumbs and forefingers formed a semi-circle under her breasts, but he hated the roughness of the denim beneath his touch, and groaned in protest.

He had no idea how she knew what he was protesting about, but she reached up, undid the buttons of her dungarees and let the material fall open—all without breaking the kiss.

He leaned back to look. She wore a crop top. Red and sleeveless, it stopped above her belly button, skimming the loveliest skin he'd ever seen. He dropped to his knees so he could get a better look. Stared in awe at the brown skin that reminded him of sand when the sun hit it just right. He traced the slight white lines of stretchmarks peeking out at her waist, where the dungarees were still held up by her hips, and he looked up so he could tell her how beautiful she was.

Her gaze was open, soft as she watched him. As she smiled a smile that travelled to his heart, settling in the heat that had been there from the start. She reached out, cupped his face, and they stayed like that for a while. Him on his knees... her staring down at him. It was something he'd always remember. He knew it in his soul. It was as if someone had taken a picture, capturing the intimacy, the specialness of the moment.

And then she reached for him, and he stood, and their mouths met again, and all the slowness of before disappeared. They kissed as if it was their final day on earth. Eager, desperate, wanting to memorise what was happening because it would likely never happen again.

Even as he had that thought he pushed it away, kissed her deeper. She gripped his top and he moved back, throwing off the offending item before pulling her top off, too. He stared at her. The sports bra she wore today flattened her breasts, and his fingers itched to pull that off, too. But there was something beautiful in the simplicity of it. And breasts were breasts—even when they were flattened.

He kissed the curves he could see, and then she was running her hands down his chest, her nails lightly tickling him, and he bit his lip, feeling the arousal of it hit him in the gut. He'd had enough. He wanted to be doing more than this.

He picked her up and pushed her against the door. Felt the air leave her body as she absorbed the impact.

'Morgan,' he said, chest heaving. 'Are you okay?'

'Yes.'

'You don't sound okay. You sound…out of breath.' He shook his head. 'I'm sorry. I shouldn't have—'

'Are you listening to yourself right now?' she interrupted. 'You're out of breath, too. Because we're…you know…'

He did know. But he had to make sure.

'We can stop,' he told her, searching her face. 'We can stop any time you want.'

'I know that. We won't have sex,' she said a little shakily. 'I… I'm not…'

'Morgan.' When she looked at him he lifted a hand, brushed her brow, her cheek, her lips with his thumb. 'I only want what you want to give me.'

'I want to give you everything.'

It was so simple, his heart ached.

'I just…'

'I know.' He kissed her forehead. 'Show me what you can give me.'

Her eyes filled with gratitude—and then with a need so fierce he felt it fill cracks inside him.

And then she did. She showed him.

And he tumbled even harder in love.

CHAPTER FIFTEEN

MORGAN HADN'T EVER brought anyone to this place.

It was special to her, and unknown to so many. Which was strange on an island as small as this. But the teenagers who lived on the island only knew of the so-called 'private' beaches that everyone knew about. The lookouts that were supposedly hidden but were actually common knowledge amongst everyone who had grown up there.

None of them had felt the need to explore as if they were desperately seeking peace. Shelter from a chaotic family.

The path was a short distance away from the estate, towards the edge of the island. The beginning of it was obscured by trees and branches, and a few meters up a collapsed tree lay over the path.

'Are we allowed to be here?' Elliott asked quietly at her side.

He was more relaxed than he'd ever been since

they'd met. Which was unsurprising, considering what they'd just done at the house.

She gave an involuntary shiver at the memory of his clever hands, his extraordinary mouth. And her heart swelled at how sweet and respectful he'd been about her reservations.

She felt stupid for still having them. For being thirty years old and still having hang-ups about sex. She was well aware that birth control worked. That it was possible to have safe sex. But she didn't feel secure enough to risk it. It made no sense, and yet she clung to it—just as her twenty-two-year-old self had. Except then the man she'd been with had stiffened, grown colder, and made her feel like she'd led him on.

It had taken this experience with Elliott for her to fully realise that *had* been how Thad had made her feel. Because Elliott hadn't. He'd followed her lead, assuring her that whatever she was comfortable with was all he wanted. And so she had given. And received. More than she had with Thad, because Elliott was more dedicated to her pleasure than Thad had ever been.

It was probably unfair to compare them. But since she'd only been with two men in this way—the few dates she'd managed to go on over the years never having got past a kiss—being unfair was natural. Necessary, even, for her to stop blaming herself.

Why did she always blame herself?

'Morgan?'

She turned her head. 'Yes?'

'Are you okay?'

'Of course.' She blinked. 'Why? Don't I look okay?'

'You were distracted,' he told her. 'You look… fine.'

A compliment? She bit her bottom lip to keep from smiling, then said, 'You're worried about us being here?'

'"Worried" isn't the word I'd use.'

'Well, most people seem to share your…hesitance, when coming here. Not many people know about this place.'

'I wonder why,' he muttered darkly, before battling through the branches of the collapsed tree.

She had done it on purpose. All so she could see him struggle. When they returned, she would show him the way around the tree, and tease him when he asked why they hadn't taken that route before.

It was immature and silly of her, but she needed that. There seemed to be a dark cloud following her around. Far enough away that she didn't have to pay attention to it just yet—and there were more important things to do…the estate, the wedding—but as soon as those distractions were gone, that cloud would burst, and everything she'd been running from would rain down on her.

The drizzling she'd experienced every now

and then with Elliott wouldn't compare. And that worried her. Because that drizzling… It had messed with her head. What would a full-blown rainstorm do to her?

It didn't help that her family would be arriving this week. Her mother had called her the day before, her excitement for the upcoming wedding clear. Hattie had been messaging her in the same vein.

She hadn't heard much from her father and brother, though that wasn't surprising. In fact, she preferred it. She didn't have to pretend that things hadn't changed in the last month. That *she* hadn't changed. They had, and she had, but she had no idea how that would look when she went back to her real life.

You control it—not them.

She stepped into the clearing as that thought came, and pushed it out of her head. This wasn't the place for those kinds of thoughts. Instead, she breathed in, her lungs expanding further than they had in a long time.

Peace.

She closed her eyes, opened her arms, and let herself be. Elliott stopped next to her and she heard his sharp intake of air. Joy spread through her, as if she had birthed this piece of nature and done something impressive.

And then she opened her eyes.

They were standing in front of a waterfall. A

small one, about four metres high, with a steady fall of water that filled the stream below. The water was clear enough for her to see the pebbles beneath it, the fish swimming in it. She had never followed the stream to see where it led. The mystery of it was far too enjoyable for her to solve it with knowledge. Besides the sound of the water and the faint crash of the ocean, the chirps and squawks of nature, it was quiet.

That quiet crept around the tension she carried in her soul, kneading it until it was flat and smooth. With an exhalation, she turned to Elliott. 'What do you think?'

'It's magnificent.'

The reverence in his voice made her want to do a happy wiggle.

'No one else knows about this?'

'I'm not sure.' Carefully, she made her way over the moss-covered stones to the edge of the stream. 'I found this the first summer I came to visit my grandmother. I haven't heard anyone talk about it, and no one has ever been here when I have. If other people know about it, they're content to keep it a secret.' She shot him a look. 'Which now includes you. You take this to your grave.'

He followed her, his mouth curved. 'You're adorable.'

Adorable?

'You're taking my reference to your death

pretty calmly,' she replied, pretending it hadn't affected her at all.

'I wouldn't have come with you to this secluded place if I was worried that you'd kill me.'

She let out a huff of laughter. 'Fair point.'

His gaze stayed on hers, skipping from amusement to…to something she didn't understand. Something intense, searching.

'What?'

'You're okay with what happened back at the house?' he asked quietly.

'I am.' Now she searched *his* expression. 'How about you?'

'I'm fine.'

He said the words so quickly she might have thought he was lying if not for the ghost of a smile on his face. She snorted at it. At the arrogance that smile showed. The confidence.

Although, to be fair, he deserved it.

The thought brought a hot flush to her body. Reminded her that she was clammy from the walk up and—other things. But there was the stream…just there. They were alone. And there was no point hiding her body after what they'd already done.

She kicked off her shoes and began to take off her dungarees.

'What are you doing?' he asked, eyes widening.

'Undressing.'

'Undressing?'

His mouth opened and closed as if he was mouthing the words to a song he knew by heart.

'I promise I'm not seducing you,' she said with an amused smile. 'Not again, anyway.'

'Not purposely,' he answered darkly.

She stuck her tongue in her cheek. 'I'd like to cool off in the stream. You can turn around if you want to.'

'I don't.'

It was a growl.

Electricity charged the air.

Was this how she'd die? Electrocution?

She considered it. What had happened at the house meant the chemistry they'd been ignoring since the night she'd fallen asleep on him was finally out in the open. They could do this. Share more intimacy. Her body ached for it. For him.

But there was a part of her that acknowledged they'd been ignoring the chemistry for a reason. They were working together. Stakes were high enough that they had to put their personal feelings aside. But beneath the working together stuff, beneath even the physical attraction, was growing a solid friendship. She didn't want to ruin that most of all.

For these few weeks she'd felt close to someone. The only person she'd ever shared that feeling with was her grandmother, but there were things she couldn't even share with Grandma

Edna. For the first time she was talking about her family. About helping her parents, taking care of her siblings.

It was a relief to speak honestly about it. To share the facts and sometimes even her feelings. Not talking about it had been her way of shielding her family. She hadn't wanted anyone to think poorly of them. Not even herself.

She had got to know herself better after talking with Elliott. And she knew *him* better, too. His favourite colour, favourite food. The days of the weeks he most dreaded and most loved. What his typical day back home looked like.

She'd pulled all that information out of him carefully, deliberately. He wasn't used to talking about himself. But those mundane things had laid a foundation for the more important things. Like the fact that he was stepping in to this project because his brother had asked. Because his father had had a heart attack. It was complicated and messy—just like her own situation. She understood his position better than anyone because of that. But it also meant she knew a relationship between them would be near impossible.

Unless things changed.

Unless *they* changed.

Unless they acted on those changes.

Her heart cracked. Just a little, but enough for her to notice it. For her to realise that her feelings for Elliott wouldn't matter if they intended on returning to their old lives. She didn't know how things would look for her…for him. It made her desperate. Desperate for this moment with him.

She pulled down the straps of her dungarees, letting them fall to her hips. In one quick movement she took off her top. Her bra followed. Then she shimmied the dungarees down over her hips. Kicked them off. Repeated the movement with her underwear, slower.

All the while, she looked at him.

Met his gaze.

Waited as his eyes followed her movements. As they glowed with the fire of desire when they rested on her face.

She knew what he saw. Her naked body, responding to him. Knew that it turned him on, too. An emotion she didn't recognise thickened her throat. Not knowing what to do with it, she turned, stepping into the stream, walking until the water deepened just beneath the waterfall.

The coldness distracted her mind, her body for a minute, and she relished the relief of it. She held her breath, sank beneath the water and stayed there until her lungs tightened. When she came back up she faced Elliott again. He was still standing there. Still watching her.

'Are you coming?' she asked hoarsely.

He grunted, but made his way down to the stream. Her eyes followed him, taking in the strength of his shoulders, his arms, his legs. He pulled off his shirt, his jeans, his underwear. She heard herself exhale, though the sound was faint beneath the thudding of her heart. He was the most beautiful man she had ever seen. His chest was broad, dusted with a scattering of dark hair that disappeared at his abs but reappeared at the base of his stomach, leading to his—

She swallowed. They'd kept some of their clothing on at the house. Their heat and passion had been too fast, too delicious to bother with complete nudity. At least, that was what she'd thought. Now she wondered if she'd been protecting herself. Looking at him like this, fully naked and aroused and beautiful, she knew she loved him. Not because of his body—although it was a work of art—but because of who he was. Because he'd chosen to share himself with her, despite how vulnerable it made him feel.

When she'd stood in front of him naked she'd felt that vulnerability, too. Sharper than ever before. It had been…overwhelming. Scary.

And he'd chosen to feel that way for her.

He must have sensed something was happening because he made his way to her slowly, leaving space between them when he stopped.

'Morgan?' he said, his voice husky, the word a question.

She closed the distance, her mouth fusing with his before she could talk herself out of it. His arms wrapped around her, pulling her against him, and he kissed her with the same urgency, the same need she'd come with to him.

It was a while after that when they lay on the rocks, staring up at the midnight-blue sky with its stars twinkling down on them. Morgan had never felt so sated. So fulfilled. So...scared.

They hadn't made love, but had done almost everything except the act. And it had been an expression of her love. If things had been different—if they'd been in a relationship and this had been intentional...if they'd been anywhere but on the island—she would have had sex with him.

Because she trusted him.

Because she loved him.

But they weren't in a relationship.

They'd just fallen into what was happening between them. The island had become an alternative reality, where their happiness was more important than what had always kept them from experiencing that happiness before.

It was a fantasy.

Fantasies never lasted.

CHAPTER SIXTEEN

'WHAT ARE YOU thinking about?' came her quiet question.

Elliott couldn't tell her. He couldn't say that touching her had awakened things in him he hadn't realised existed. That kissing her had filled him. That sharing the intimacy they'd just shared had shifted things so completely he didn't know how to move on, how to move forward.

But he couldn't lie to her either.

'You,' he said, playing with the wet strands of her hair lying across her chest. 'Us.'

'Yeah?' She lifted her head, resting her chin on his chest. 'How's that going for you?'

He could hear the teasing in her voice, and the raw emotion he'd seen on her face in the stream had disappeared beneath a mask. Things must have changed for her, too. If he'd had the courage, he would have asked how. But he didn't. He was a coward, unable to face situations that were difficult. He'd done it with his family; he would do it with her. He knew that.

But for now there was this. Them. And he'd cling to the moment for as long as he could.

'It's good,' he answered.

Her expression softened and she pressed a kiss to his chest. 'You're awfully charming, Mr Abel.'

He snorted. 'Only you would think that.'

'Hmm…'

She lay back, on the rocks this time, and for a while there were only the sounds of the waterfall, the animals, the ocean. Despite his promise to himself earlier, his mind spun with thoughts. What would happen when they left this place? Would they go back to who they'd been before this night? Or would they become something he didn't recognise?

It's not good,' she said, her voice clear. Her meaning clear. 'You're worried.'

'Aren't you?'

'I'd be a fool not to be.'

And you aren't a fool.

There weren't many things about Morgan he didn't like. But one of them would certainly be how clearly she saw him. And how obscured her view of herself was.

'It wouldn't be your fault,' he said quietly. 'If things…changed.'

'Wouldn't it?'

He straightened, looked at her. Her hair was spread over the rocks, curling wildly, glowing faintly in the moonlight. She'd put her clothes back on, but her dungarees were pulled down to her waist, so that he could see the red crop top. She was as beautiful like this as she had been naked and vulnerable before him.

His heart begged him to reconsider, making him realise he'd already decided to push her away. But it was for the best. He'd rather hurt her now than down the line, when she realised he could never be what she wanted.

The wind rustled. He looked at her again, this time noticing her nipples had pebbled underneath her top and her skin was gooseflesh.

'You're cold,' he said.

'You're scared,' she replied.

Oh, he *did* hate how clearly she saw him. But he wouldn't deny it. 'You are, too.'

'Worried…scared,' she confirmed. 'You've turned me into someone who thinks about her life. I haven't done that. Not in a long time. And now I want—' She broke off. Sat up. Wrapped her arms around her legs. 'What I want doesn't matter.'

'It does.'

'No, it doesn't. I have a real life to go back to. Spending nights with you under the moonlight isn't real.'

'But it could be.'

Why had he said that? It had leapt from his lips, directly from his heart, and now she was looking at him with wide eyes. Wide, *hopeful* eyes.

Then she shook her head. 'No, it can't be. What happens when we go back? My family…they still need me. And yours…' She trailed off, looking at him. 'I don't even know how to answer that, Elliott. And doesn't that mean we're bound to fail?'

No.

But he wouldn't say it. He wouldn't give her hope again, only to witness it being snuffed out. As it had to be.

'You're right,' he said roughly. 'It's not because of you.'

'Why do you keep saying that?'

'Because you don't see it.'

'See *what*?' she snapped. 'This started because of me. Right from the moment I tricked you into meeting with me that first day.'

'This is what I mean. You take responsibility when you shouldn't.'

'If I don't, who else will?'

She stood, tied the straps of her dungarees. Elliott vaguely recalled the beginning of the night. When she'd untied them and everything had felt beautiful and hopeful.

He'd spoiled that.

No, he thought. He couldn't believe that if he didn't want her to believe it.

'I know why you think that,' he said quietly. 'You've been responsible for your family for as long as you can remember. But that doesn't mean you should be. Your parents are adults. Your siblings are, too.' He paused. 'Maybe it's time you let them take responsibility for themselves, Morgan.'

'Really?' Her tone was sarcastic. 'I did that once, remember? My sister was hysterical and my parents were—'

'Morgan,' he said again, 'you don't owe them your life.'

'That's what you don't get!' she exclaimed, throwing up her hands. 'I do. I *do*. My parents' lives changed because they had me. They sacrificed so much. So I…' She folded her arms, shivering in the wind that had gone cold. 'The least I could do was make it easy for them.'

He'd known what her situation with her family was, but he hadn't expected this. A guilt that made no sense, and yet was perfectly sensible when it came to her. When it came to family. She hadn't expected to tell him either, it seemed, because her eyes widened and filled.

Instinctively he stepped forward, his arms open. She stepped back, shaking her head.

'I'm sorry,' she hiccuped. 'I just…' She shook her head again, more vehemently. Then, deliberately, she inhaled. Blew out air. Squared her shoulders. 'We should probably get back.'

He followed her wordlessly, down the steep decline that forced his focus to the path. When she led him around the fallen tree she'd previously led him through, he didn't comment. If it had been a couple of hours earlier he would have.

He would have asked her about it. Likely been teased about it, too.

But a couple of hours earlier things had been easier between them. Inside himself.

She hadn't meant to reject him. Still, it stung. Reminded him of all the times in his childhood when he'd followed his instincts and been pushed away despite that.

Because of it?

He took a breath. No, this wasn't about him. If Morgan had known what he was thinking—if she had been thinking clearly—she would have told him that, too. He knew that as well as he knew that his own issues were blinding him. That they were the reason he couldn't be with her in the first place.

How could he know that and still be so helpless to stop it?

Not helpless, a voice that sounded alarmingly like Morgan's echoed in his head. *Unwilling.*

Unwilling?

He was immensely grateful that they'd arrived back at the estate then, because the scene in front of him demanded all his attention.

'Morgan!' Edna pushed through the small crowd of people who'd been standing outside the house he and Morgan had been working on. 'Morgan, thank goodness you're all right!'

'Of course I'm all right. I just— *Ow! Gran!* Why did you *do* that?'

'Because you didn't come home!' Edna emphasised each word with another poke to Morgan's chest. 'You didn't come home, you didn't leave a message, and you weren't answering your phone.'

'I'm a grown-up!' Morgan exclaimed, shifting so that his body was in front of hers.

She was using him as a shield.

It would have amused him if he hadn't been afraid Edna would start poking him, too.

'A grown-up lets the people around her know that she's okay!'

'Honestly, Gran, what did you think? There's virtually no crime around here. And I was with Elliott.'

Edna's eyes narrowed to slits as they rested on Elliott.

'Elliott,' she growled. 'What were you doing with my granddaughter?'

He had absolutely no answer for that.

'It better have been something sexy,' someone said from behind Edna. 'I think Edna would be able to forgive you if it were something sexy.'

There was a long pause as everyone in the crowd—people he knew and didn't know— watched them expectantly.

'I could,' Edna said a beat later. 'I could forgive you if it were something sexy.'

'The *people* on this island—I swear!'

With those words, Morgan stormed off.

They all stared after her. Then, slowly, people looked at him.

'No,' he said.

He had no desire to share what had happened with these people. Even if he did feel more connected to this community than he had anywhere before.

The thought stayed with him throughout the short drive home—as did thoughts about Morgan. Memories, good and bad, of everything they'd shared tonight. They distracted him. Twirling in his head. Mocking him. Teasing him. So much so that when he parked in his driveway he didn't realise there was another car there until it was too late.

By then his brother had already seen him.

CHAPTER SEVENTEEN

MORGAN WENT THROUGH variations of what she would tell Elliott when she saw him that morning.

I overreacted.

I shouldn't have said what I said.

I'm sorry we can't be together.

The last one was what she really wanted to say. She *was* sorry. After everything they'd been through—particularly everything they'd shared the day before—all she wanted was for them to be together. But it was impossible.

He'd made her see that her issues ran deeper than even she had thought. She'd had no idea she'd been making herself smaller because she felt guilty. She'd had no idea the real reason she'd helped raise her siblings was because she'd wanted to make it up to her parents.

It wasn't right, and it wasn't healthy. She could recognise that. But it twisted her insides. She hadn't been able to sleep the night before, trying to think it through. When it had become clear that wouldn't be possible she'd tried not to think about it at all—and had ended up thinking about Elliott instead.

She'd hurt him, even though they both knew they had no future together. They both wanted one, though. That much was clear. If things were simple, if the world were an easier place, that would be enough.

Why couldn't that be enough?

Her phone rang, distracting her. She opened it to find a message from Elliott, telling her he wouldn't be coming to the estate that day. Her shoulders stiffened, her stomach tightened, but she sent back an acknowledgement—a thumbs-up emoji, because she had no words—and began on the finishing touches of one of the last houses they had to do.

She wasn't angry at him for not coming. She understood it on a personal level. But they still had to work together. She'd hoped he'd manage to set aside his feelings so that they would be able to complete the project. And fear that he might not was the reason she hadn't wanted them to give in to their desires. Part of the reason, anyway. The other part was that she'd always known giving in would bring them to this. Sad, broken, without even the friendship they'd forged over the last weeks.

Every instinct told her this was her fault. She had been the one to make the first move the night before. She'd taken off her clothes at the stream, offered herself to him. But he'd accepted her; offered her the same. It hadn't been easy for him, and still he'd done it. And he'd told her it wasn't her fault. That they'd both made the decision and that meant they shared the responsibility.

Was that true for her family as well?

She straightened, leaving the carpet she'd been putting down half unrolled. *Could* she apply this to her family? No, that didn't work. Her siblings hadn't asked Morgan to look after them—Morgan had made that decision. In the same way her parents hadn't asked Morgan to make their job easier. Morgan had made that decision, too.

Oh.

Oh.

She *had* made those decisions. The situation with her family was what it was because *she'd* crafted it that way. She'd assumed responsibility because of her own feelings. But, in the same breath, they'd allowed her to. It might not have been an intentional decision, but her parents had encouraged Morgan's obedience, accepted her help.

It was trickier with her siblings, because that was all they'd ever known. But her parents? That situation was a little simpler. And if she was assigning responsibility for decisions more fairly, it had been her parents' decision to have her. They had chosen to go through with the pregnancy. They had chosen to raise her. She would always be grateful for their sacrifices, but perhaps…perhaps her gratitude could be shown in another way.

After decades, maybe she could finally stop trying to make up for her birth.

Maybe…maybe she didn't have to.

'Morgan?'

She whirled around, clamping her hand over her chest as she tried to calm her heart.

'Elliott,' she said, her knees going weak at the sight of him.

That was just because of the shock, she was sure.

No, it's because you love him.

'I'm sorry.' He shoved his hands into his pockets. 'Didn't mean to scare you.'

'No.' It was a quick response. As if responding quickly would allow her to escape that thought. All her thoughts. 'It's not your fault. I was distracted.' She cleared her throat. 'I thought you weren't coming,' she accused softly.

If he hadn't come she could have pretended her feelings for him had been amplified by the moonlight. She wouldn't have had to see his handsome face, all stormy and closed off from her—and yet still so breathtaking. He was wearing T-shirt and jeans again, and they moulded to every muscle she had admired, touched, the night before.

She'd lain her head on his chest, heard his heartbeat, and felt closer to him than to any other person. She'd kissed him, tasted him, shared the sweetest intimacy with him. Physical intimacy. Emotional intimacy. It was because of him that she was realising things could be different with her family.

She was standing on the precipice of a new life. If he hadn't come she could have pretended she didn't want that life to include him.

'I…' He stepped through the door, and for the first time she saw that he wasn't alone. 'This is my brother—Gio. Gio, this is Morgan. She's been co-ordinating the estate revamp.'

It was as if someone had cloned Elliott, with a few key differences. His brother was shorter, stockier. He had a beard, lighter eyes, and he wore glasses. But he was just as handsome as his brother, and much less still.

Gio walked forward, smiling politely at her, and offered his hand. 'It's nice to meet you, Morgan.'

Morgan took his hand, her eyes flickering to Elliott. He was watching them with an unreadable expression on his face. 'It's nice to meet you, too.'

'Hard to believe that this is the first time we've interacted, considering you're running point on this project.'

The words put her back up. 'Technically, your brother's running point. I've worked with many project managers, and Elliott's one of the best.'

It wasn't a lie, but from the corner of her eye she saw Elliott stiffen.

Gio frowned. 'With all due respect, you're hardly qualified to make that evaluation.'

Her brows rose. She looked at Elliott. 'You didn't tell him who I am?'

Elliott grunted.

She sighed. 'Mr Abel—Gio?' Gio nodded. 'Gio, my name is Morgan Simeon. I'm a property expert. Which means I—'

'Morgan Simeon?' Gio interrupted. 'Why does that name sound familiar?' His eyes widened. 'You worked on the Lando Project.'

'Yes, I was responsible for that.'

'It's amazing. Some of the best work I've seen. Which I'm sure you know is a compliment, coming from me.'

Cocky, this brother. But, since she did know it was a compliment, she smiled. 'Thank you.'

'How did Elliott manage to get you here?'

Her smile faded at the incredulity in his voice. 'Happy coincidence. Now, I'm sure you have questions. And I'd be happy to answer them. But, as I told you, your brother's been responsible for most of the work.'

As if he'd been waiting for that moment, Gio began firing questions at them. Well, at her. Despite her suggestion that he ask his brother, Gio chose not to. And Morgan soon grew tired of it. She diverted the questions to Elliott, and he— grudgingly—answered.

His answers were good, though there were

times when she wanted to interject. She resisted the temptation. If she did that she would undermine him, and Gio had just started actually directing his questions to Elliott—just as grudgingly as his brother had begun to answer them earlier.

At the end of it, Gio folded his arms. 'I'm impressed, E. If this pans out—and it seems like it will—you'll have saved us time and money. No small amount of either.' Gio studied his brother. 'But if you'd answered my emails I wouldn't have had to fly all the way here for this conversation.'

'He's humble,' Morgan said when Elliott's expression closed up. 'And emails wouldn't have given you a chance to speak with me and inspect the work yourself.'

Gio smiled. It was a nice smile. An easy smile. Elliott's was neither.

She preferred Elliott's.

She preferred Elliott.

'I haven't seen as much as I'd like to,' Gio said slowly, 'but what I have seen has impressed me. You wouldn't by any chance be interested in a job, Ms Simeon? I could make you a lucrative offer.'

'You'd have to do more than that to get me to give up the business I've built my entire adult life,' Morgan said with a huff of laughter. 'But I'm flattered.' She became aware of Elliott's gaze, hot and intense, focused directly on her. 'I'll give you my card, Gio. Maybe we can find a way to work together minus the part where you become my boss.'

She handed him one of the cards she kept in her wallet and then pretended to see a message on her phone that required her attention. She made her excuses, claiming that she needed to check on something in the garden, and hightailed it out of the room.

Minutes later, her brain caught up with her legs. She'd walked further than she intended. Past her car, past the houses she needed to check on, past the garden she'd claimed to be going to. She was almost at the beach when Elliott caught her up.

'Morgan.'

He wasn't out of breath when he said it, which was, frankly, rude since he must have run. She'd *walked* and she was breathing faster than usual.

'Why are you here?' she asked. 'Your brother must want you to show him the estate.'

'You lied.'

'I did not.'

'You told him I was responsible for the estate.'

'You are.'

'No, I'm not.'

When she didn't reply, he reached out and caught her wrist. He let go as soon as she stopped.

'We did it together.'

'I'm trying not to take responsibility where I

don't have to,' she said. It felt as if she'd tossed the words in the air, not caring where they fell. 'It's not important for your brother to know that I helped you with this. It *is* important that he knows about *your* part in it. You've played a huge part, Elliott. The time and money he's saving is because you decided to renovate instead of rebuild.'

He didn't answer. Only stared at her with a deep frown. His brain was spinning. She could all but see it in his eyes. It stung, as she remembered the time when she hadn't been able to read him. Now he was like her favourite book.

She started walking again.

'Morgan,' he growled. 'You can't say something like that and walk away.'

'Yes, I can.'

He jogged up to her side, and then sped up and stopped ahead of her.

'Stop.'

'No.'

'Morgan.'

'Elliott?'

'Morgan.'

She stopped. 'I don't want to talk about this.'

'Why not?'

'Because you don't see yourself. Or you hide yourself. Either way, nothing I say is going to change that.'

Emotion flickered in his eyes. It softened her,

and so she walked until she was in front of him and cupped his face.

'You're kind. Thoughtful. Someone with power who chooses to help those without it. You're smart. You've built a successful company from scratch. You did all of that—' she pointed in the direction of the estate '—on your own terms. Why you don't see how capable you are...' She shook her head, dropping her hands. 'I don't even have to answer that. I know why. I saw it back there with your brother.'

He exhaled. 'He's the smart one.'

'Elliott,' she said, resisting the urge to smack him. 'Just because your brother's smart, it doesn't mean you aren't! People can have the same qualities.'

'Not in my family.' He shoved his hands into his pockets again. The same thing he'd done back at the estate. It meant he was feeling vulnerable, she realised. 'You were either my brother, or...'

'You weren't good enough?' she asked when he didn't finish.

'Or you were me.'

She breathed in carefully, exhaled slowly, even as she was plotting the deaths of all the people who'd made this beautiful, brilliant man feel that way. Words formed in her head, almost spilled from her lips, but she pulled them back. Went through them carefully because she knew whatever she said would have an impact.

'Do you trust me?' she asked quietly.

He gave an imperceptible nod.

'Good.' It *was* good, but that wasn't a thought for now. 'If you trust me, you have to believe what I've said. I meant every word, Elliott. You're a good person. The best person.' *My person.* She swallowed. 'And I see you. I see you for who you are. I see you better than you see yourself.'

He clenched his jaw, looked out at the waves. It was done on purpose, so she couldn't see his face, and she gave him his privacy. Waited until he'd worked through it. Hoped that he trusted her enough to listen.

But when he looked at her she could see the fight on his face. The disbelief. Her heart, already showing signs of wear, crumbled. She didn't want him to feel this way. She wanted him to feel confident. Proud. She wanted him to believe in the mask he showed the world. To believe in himself.

She let out a shaky breath, stood on her toes and kissed his cheek. Then she turned and walked away.

'This isn't fair,' he said at her side.

He'd followed her.

'No, it's not,' she agreed. 'But that doesn't matter.'

'Please.' His voice was gruff. 'Try to understand.'

She stopped. Looked at him. 'I can't understand what I don't know.'

His chest was heaving. Up, down…up, down… In a steady rhythm despite its speed.

And then he spoke.

'You do know. You know what it's like to turn yourself into something because you want your family's love and acceptance.'

The words went off like a gong in her head. It was true; she knew it. Still, it echoed, ringing in her ears until he continued.

'I spent half my life doing that. All it ever did was make me feel…incapable. Not good enough,' he said, using her earlier words. 'Getting my parents' love shouldn't have been that hard. I knew that, and still I tried. Eventually I got tired of it. I refused to let people's opinions affect the way I saw myself.'

'Including mine?'

His eyes met hers. 'Yes.'

She pursed her lips. 'That's fine. Admirable, even. The only problem is that you see yourself the way you believe they see you. No?' she asked when he frowned. 'You let your brother walk all over you. That's not the Elliott I've got to know. And when Gio did eventually give you your due, you didn't accept it. You didn't *believe* it. Just like you don't believe me.'

It hurt, but this wasn't about her. It would never be about her, about them, until he saw the truth. Maybe she'd known that all along.

'You don't have to believe him. Or me, for that

matter. Just believe the work you've put into your life over this second half of it. Look at yourself, at your achievements. Look at the warehouse full of your furniture. Look at the estate.' She paused. 'And when you're done, look at me. At us. At the relationships you've built with the people in this community. There's a whole new life waiting for you if you look and *see*. If you stop pushing people away. If you just…' She exhaled. 'If you just believed in yourself.'

This time when she walked away she didn't turn back.

And he didn't follow.

CHAPTER EIGHTEEN

'LOOK AT ME. At us... There's a whole new life waiting for you if you look and see.'

Elliott couldn't get those words out of his head. Had she been saying he had the chance at a life with her? If she had been, would that change anything? Would he be able to do what she was asking?

The fact that he couldn't answer told him all he needed to know.

Slowly, he made his way back to the estate. His brother had continued the tour without him, and he found Gio in the garden, chatting with Thad. Elliott paused. Watched them. Tried to figure out how his worlds had collided in this strange, incomprehensible way. He had no answers—it seemed to be the day for it—so he hung back, waited for Gio to finish, all the while thinking about what Morgan had said.

He didn't want to think about what Morgan had said. Her words threatened everything about his life. Because they'd pointed out precisely how carefully he had crafted that life. Throwing himself into work so he didn't have to think about his feelings. Not engaging in any meaningful relationships for the same reason. If he'd given himself the time to think about those feelings—if he'd allowed people into his life who would have made him think about those feelings—he wouldn't be where he was now.

Confused. Hurt. Sad.

But he wasn't that person any more. That little boy who'd felt those emotions all the time. Who'd allowed those emotions to drive him. He didn't want any of that—but he wanted Morgan. And, unlike his family, she seemed to want him, too.

His eyes fell on Gio. Maybe he wasn't being entirely fair towards his family. Gio had asked him to help with the project. Surely he wouldn't have done that if he didn't trust Elliott? If he thought Elliott incapable? He'd complimented Elliott, too. Yes, it had come after some dismissal, but that might have been because Elliott had always allowed it. Encouraged it, in fact.

Over the years Elliott had chosen to let his family think what they wanted. On the odd occasion when they saw one another they treated him like the person who'd been written about in the newspapers. A furniture tycoon. A playboy. And he'd allowed it because it was easier to let them reject that version of him than reject who he actually was.

His brother didn't know who he actually was.

No one did—except Morgan.

Perhaps he needed to change that.

'Elliott?'

Gio was staring at him expectantly. It took Elliott a second to realise his brother was standing in front of him.

'What?'

'We can go.'

Elliott nodded in reply. He drove back to the house in silence. Once there, he unlocked the door and went straight to the fridge. He stared at the meals he'd defrosted. There were plenty more in the freezer. Proof, he thought. It might be part of their generosity as a community, but the people of Penguin Island had gone out of their way for him. Proof that he was a part of something. That he meant something to them.

And they had come to mean something to him, too.

'Okay, this is getting ridiculous,' Gio said.

Elliott turned, surprised to find him hovering a few steps away.

'What is going on with you? You've been distracted since we left the estate.'

'Sorry,' he muttered. Then he thought, *Screw it*. 'Did you mean what you said back there? That you're impressed with the plans for the estate?'

'Yeah.' Gio frowned. 'Why wouldn't I mean it?'

He shrugged. 'I don't know you well enough to know when you're lying.'

'And you think I'd lie about this?' The frown deepened. Gio folded his arms and leaned against the counter. 'This is because of Mom and Dad, isn't it?'

Elliott's heart skipped. He gave a quick nod, and half hoped his brother hadn't noticed.

Of course he'd noticed.

'Yeah, I guess a lot of your stuff is because of Mom and Dad...' Gio exhaled. 'Mine is, too.'

'Yours?'

Gio's brows lifted. 'What? You don't think our parents screwed me up, too?'

He didn't know what to say to that.

'I guess that's fair.' Gio straightened and went to the fridge, taking out one of the meals Elliott had been staring at. 'I haven't really spoken about it. Not to you, at least. You want some of this?'

Elliott could barely keep up with the conversation. He said yes to the question, though he wasn't really hungry, then waited for Gio to say more.

'It's always been a ton of pressure to be the genius in the family.' Gio slid the food into the microwave and pressed 'start'. 'They expected me to act like one. But I didn't know how to act like a genius, only myself, and that didn't seem good enough for them. Ironic, considering acting like myself meant acting like a genius.'

'But they've always been so proud of you.'

'Yeah…' He didn't speak for a while. 'Did you ever know how jealous I was of you? They let you do whatever you wanted. You had a freedom I'd never got and…' Gio's mouth twisted. 'I wanted it. I wanted to be you. You left home after school and you didn't look back. What was that like?'

It took Elliott a second to realise Gio was really asking. Then he said, 'Lonely.'

Gio's gaze didn't leave Elliott's face. For once Elliott didn't care about what Gio saw there.

He wasn't surprised when his brother said, 'You felt the same way about me, didn't you? You wanted to be me.'

'I wanted them to…love me.'

'They do love you.'

'Maybe.' His mind was spinning with Gio's confession. With the fact that he'd made his own. And, since he had, there seemed no point in keeping this next part to himself. 'But not in any way that matters.'

The microwave beeped in the silence. Gio was still watching him. After a few minutes his brother took out the food, shared it between the two plates he'd got out earlier, and took two beers from the fridge.

'How about we talk, brother?' Gio asked as he slid the meal over to Elliott. 'I think we could both do with an honest conversation.'

The morning of the wedding, Elliott woke up early. The last week had been a blur of final preparations. They'd managed to get all the houses ready on time for the guests who were staying there, and Morgan had pulled some strings to ensure the final inspections had been done on time. It had literally taken until the day before, with him, his brother and Morgan burying themselves in work.

Gio had readily agreed to stay and help when he'd learned about the wedding, although Elliott suspected it had less to do with the wedding and more to do with him. That 'honest conversation' Gio had wanted to have had been…illuminating. They'd both told each other something about what they'd felt growing up—not everything, but enough to get an idea—and somehow that had created a bond between them. It was new and tentative, and neither he nor his brother was entirely comfortable with it, but it was there. It was important.

For now, that was enough.

He couldn't believe it. His brother…wanting a relationship with him. Every instinct told him not to trust it. It would disappear, and then what would happen? He'd be hurt again and he'd go back to his old life.

Except nothing would really change in his life. At least not in the life he'd created in Cape Town. If Gio did something to break their fragile bond it wouldn't affect Elliott. He'd go back to running his business. Back to only seeing his family on special occasions. Yes, he'd be hurt—but wasn't a relationship with his brother worth the risk? Because if Gio *didn't* let him down, Elliott would finally have some semblance of a family. And wasn't that what he'd always wanted?

He would have given anything to talk it through with Morgan, but she'd been treating him coolly since the last time they'd spoken. That was fair. He'd pushed her away and she was responding in kind. Fair, he thought again, but not harmless. It hurt. But then, he seemed to be in a place where hurt was inevitable. It scared the life out of him, and yet it seemed hopeful.

Hope. He hadn't experienced that in years. He supposed that was what happened when someone fell in love.

He showered, left a note for his brother, and went to help with the last-minute preparations. The café that had become his and Morgan's unofficial meeting spot every morning was normally closed at this time of day, but today they let him in. Morgan was already there. Seemed they'd opened early for her, too. And they'd given her breakfast. An untouched croissant along with coffee.

He gestured to the server for coffee of his own and went to join her. She didn't look at him. Instead, she kept on staring into the distance. He followed her gaze, saw there was nothing there, and then waited to see if she'd notice him.

It took the delivery of his coffee to draw her out of her thoughts.

'Hey,' she said, blinking a few times as her eyes came into focus. 'How long have you been here?'

'You need a fresh cup of coffee,' he replied, nodding at the server. 'You're nervous.'

'What? No. I'm just…distracted.'

'What's happened?'

'Nothing.' She dipped her finger into the cold coffee, winced, and pulled her finger out. 'Urgh. I really have been here too long.'

He waited.

She sighed. 'It's annoying when you do that.'

'But it works.'

Her lips curved and she shook her head. 'Nothing's happened. I just need to breathe before the day starts.' She paused. 'My family got in last night.'

He searched her face, looking for any sign that they'd done something to upset her. She looked… strained. And distracted, as she'd said. But she didn't seem angry or upset.

'Are you okay?' he asked for good measure.

'I'm fine. No, that's not true.' She immediately contradicted herself. 'I need to have an honest conversation with them and I… I don't know how to do it.' There was a beat. 'Maybe I am nervous, after all. How did you know?'

'I know you.'

He didn't know if that was the right thing to say, considering how things were between them. But she just nodded, looked out of the window. As if what he'd said was true. As if she'd accepted it.

Hope bloomed inside him.

'Honest conversations aren't that bad,' he said.

'Aren't they?' Her tone was dry. 'I recall several of ours being catastrophic.'

He grunted. The server brought her coffee.

A few seconds later, she said, 'Are you talking about you and your brother?'

He nodded.

'You told him? About the stuff with your parents?'

He nodded again.

She bit her lip. 'How did he respond?'

'Well…' He cleared his throat. 'He…he has some issues, too.'

This time she nodded. She ran a finger around the rim of her coffee cup, a smile playing on her face. She was happy for him.

Of course she's happy for you. She loves you.

He didn't know that. He didn't know that at all. And he refused to entertain the thought until he did.

'He asked me to offer you a job again,' Elliott said into the silence.

'He's already offered it to me three times. Your offer makes it a fourth.'

Elliott couldn't blame Gio. Her work on the

estate was impeccable. She'd turned viewing several somewhat unremarkable houses into a striking, cohesive experience. Flipper Estate could easily compete with other top-rated beach-side estates now, and she'd managed that with straightforward reconstruction and clever design. The garden was a triumph, too, although she'd had little to do with that. It didn't matter. Her contributions made it clear she deserved to be called an expert.

'Will you consider it?'

'Not a job, no. A partnership, maybe.'

'He'll be disappointed.'

'I think he'll survive,' she answered dryly.

She began to eat her croissant, breaking it apart and leaving flakes all over her plate. He waited for her to say something else, but she didn't. That told him just how tense things were between them. Morgan liked to talk. She had from the moment he'd met her. He hadn't realised how much he liked it when she filled the silences until now, when she didn't.

He'd never really cared for small talk, but he found himself doing it anyway. 'Did you like him?'

'Who?'

'Gio.'

She brought her cup to her lips. 'I've liked him more since he's started giving you the credit you deserve.'

'He likes you,' he answered softly, and then continued with something he'd had no idea he'd been thinking about. 'And his fascination isn't only professional.'

Her brow furrowed. 'Are you flirting with me on your brother's behalf?'

'No.'

'No...' she repeated, her eyes searching, seeing too much. She sat back, her hands still around the cup. 'In case it isn't clear, my feelings for your brother are entirely dependent on you. He's been treating you better, so I like him better.' She set her coffee on the table. 'I'm a little offended that you think I might reciprocate whatever fascination he has for me beyond professionalism.'

Up until she'd asked that question about flirting, he hadn't been aware of his jealousy. He'd watched the ease with which Morgan and Gio interacted and he'd...he'd internalised it. Now he could see that he'd been bracing himself for her to tell him she preferred Gio. That she'd compared him with his brother and found him lacking. The fact that she hadn't—that she'd based her entire opinion of Gio on his treatment of Elliott—told him that she cared about him.

And that he needed to get a grip on his issues.

'I'm sorry. It's...it's not you.'

'I know that,' she snapped. Then she gave a frustrated exhalation. 'But honestly it *should* be about me. You know me better than anyone, Elliott. You know how I feel about you. I wish you'd trust that.'

He was about to reply when Sharon stormed in, eyes wide, chest heaving.

Morgan was at her side immediately, Elliott not far behind. 'What? What's happened?'

'Edna,' Sharon panted. 'She's gone.'

'Gone?' Morgan repeated. 'What do you mean "gone"?'

'She's not at the house and no one can find her.'

CHAPTER NINETEEN

SOMETIMES WHEN MORGAN couldn't sleep, she'd go through the wedding day in her head. She'd think about how beautiful her grandmother would look, how stunning the garden would be, how everyone would gaze upon the couple with joy and celebrate their union of love.

Not once had Morgan considered a runaway bride.

'We'll have to cancel,' Joyce said.

All her grandmother's friends had arrived shortly after Sharon, with assurances that the only people who knew what had happened were those in the room. They'd yet to tell Stanley, who was still peacefully asleep in one of the other houses on the estate, her grandmother having insisted they not see one another until the wedding day.

No. There was no way her grandmother had run away from him.

'We're not cancelling,' Morgan said.

'We have no bride,' Joyce pointed out.

'We have a bride. She's just…not here right now.'

'And do you know where she might be?'

'No,' Morgan replied, 'but I know my grandmother. She would not leave her fiancé at the altar.'

'I don't know, dear,' Clarice said. 'Edna loves drama. Some of her favourite movies are about jilted grooms.'

Morgan resisted the urge to roll her eyes. 'I'd bet an organ that that isn't what's happening here.' Something occurred to her. 'Has any one of you actually *looked* for her?'

There was a beat.

'Well, not physically,' Sharon said. 'We've all tried to call her, but her phone's off.'

'So when you said "no one can find her" you meant what, exactly?'

A strange sound came from her left. When she turned, Elliott had his hand over his face and was pretending not to laugh.

She narrowed her eyes. 'Find this amusing, do you?'

He held up both hands in surrender, his lips twitching. Now she did roll her eyes, and then turned back to her grandmother's friends.

'I'm beginning to think Grandma Edna isn't the one who loves drama.'

'Excuse me?' Sharon huffed, straightening her spine.

'Morgan,' Joyce said. 'That's just rude.'

'Not untrue,' Clarice added with a sniff, 'but definitely impolite.'

The bell on the door sounded and they all turned with smiles on their faces as if nothing was wrong.

Edna stared back at them. 'What's going on here? You all look insanely suspicious.'

As her friends flocked to her, admonishing her for switching off her phone, demanding her whereabouts, Morgan hung back. She felt Elliott at her side long before he spoke.

'How did you know she hadn't run?'

'She loves Stanley.'

She watched her grandmother laugh and roll her eyes at her friends, her face bright and happy, the most joyous Morgan had ever seen her.

'I think, for her, it's the simplest thing. She loves him. She wants to be with him. She wouldn't do anything that would mean they can't be together.'

She looked at Elliott now, her breath catching at the look of intensity on his face. Her words replayed in her head, and she realised that maybe it *was* simple. If she loved Elliott she would do what she needed to do so they could be together. He would, too. But she couldn't control his actions—heaven knew she'd tried. Tried to get him to see himself...to see her. The truth was that he needed to see them, too.

She could see them. She could see their future

together. And that meant that she needed to make things simple. Which involved facing her worst fears. But she could do it. She *would* do it. For herself *and* for them.

'I'll see you later?' she asked him quietly.

He nodded. She did, too. Then she turned before she could linger. Before she could cup his face, kiss his lips, tell him her plans.

Her grandmother left with her, and they walked back to the estate.

'That was an exciting start to the morning,' Edna commented.

Morgan laughed. 'Not quite what you imagined for the morning of your wedding.'

Her grandmother didn't answer. Morgan narrowed her eyes suspiciously and saw her suspicions confirmed.

'You *wanted* that to happen?' she accused her.

'I wanted some excitement.'

'Your wedding almost had to be cancelled. Why wasn't that enough excitement for you?'

'Oh, I stopped worrying about that the moment I called you.'

Morgan chose not to address that. 'How did you even know your friends would react that way?'

'They love drama.'

'As do you, apparently.'

Edna winked at her, and she couldn't help but laugh.

'You're a hypocrite,' Morgan informed her. 'You nearly had a heart attack when you didn't hear from me the other night, and then you do the same thing to your friends.'

'Yes, well, I'm your grandmother. I have a right to hypocrisy.'

'Is that what you tell yourself?'

'Yes.'

She snorted again.

They walked in silence for a bit, and then Edna said, 'Have you told him you love him yet?'

Morgan nearly stumbled. 'What? Who? No.'

'Darling,' Edna said, in the gentlest tone, 'you do realise that I have eyes in my head?'

She opened her mouth, but her grandmother was still talking.

'I can't remember the last time you smiled the way you do when he's around. You don't ever do things like sneak around and not let your grandmother know where you are. You didn't even do that with Thad,' Edna added. 'Even when you sneaked around with him, you'd give me an itinerary. Fake, but still… I knew where you were.' She paused. 'Where did you go that night with Elliott?'

'Gran…' Morgan huffed in protest, bothered by her grandmother's revelations, but not enough to sacrifice her privacy.

'Fine, fine.' Edna waved a hand. 'Don't tell me.

I'm sure I don't really want to know.' She took a deep breath. 'Morgan, you never do anything for yourself. *Never*. Elliott's been helping you with that. You should tell him that you love him.'

'That's… Gran…'

'You think I haven't seen it?' Edna asked, cutting off her stammering. 'I have. I've intervened when I can with your parents, but you've always seemed content with the way things are. And then you haven't been—not in the last few years. So I decided that I would finally accept Stanley's proposal and we'd move to Cape Town. We'd help with Hattie and Rob, give you some space to figure out what you want. But I knew you'd need a kick in the butt, so I asked you to come here. To help me.'

Morgan's jaw dropped.

Finally. Finally it made sense why her grandmother had called her. Edna had never asked for Morgan's help. Not once. Morgan had assumed it was because Edna's life was exactly the way she wanted it. Edna was sharp, smart about her decisions, and she was happy to live with the consequences when things didn't work out.

It was for that very reason that Morgan had jumped on a plane when Edna had called. She'd thought things must be serious if Edna was reaching out to her.

That part was probably still true. Only it was Morgan's life that had needed the intervention.

Also—Edna had spoken to her parents about this?

'Gran,' Morgan said slowly. 'How are you only telling me this now?'

'Would you have listened if I'd told you before?' Edna didn't wait for an answer. 'I'm quite pleased with the way things have turned out. I only meant to get you to the island for a break. I didn't think you would meet Elliott, let alone fall in love with him. That was an unexpected bonus.'

She sounded giddy.

'This is a lot to take in…'

'Oh, don't be angry. I'm your grandmother. I have a right to interfere in your life.'

'I thought we went through this?' Morgan muttered darkly.

'We did,' her grandmother said cheerfully. 'I made an executive decision.'

Morgan couldn't help her laugh. It displaced some of her tension, causing it to flutter through her body. Her stomach felt jittery, as did her heart—which wasn't great on top of the nerves she already had, knowing she needed to speak with her family. But this jitteriness wasn't bad. It was…relief. Someone in her family had seen what she was going through. Someone had *cared*. Hell, her grandmother had decided to move back to Cape Town for her.

It wasn't something she would ever have thought to ask. Grandma Edna had done so much for Morgan already. All those summers Morgan had come to the island, all the times Morgan's parents would call and Edna would fly over immediately to help.

Morgan could see now that she'd tried to relieve her grandmother of that responsibility, too. If she could look after Hattie and Rob—if her parents didn't have to call Grandma Edna—then her grandmother wouldn't see Morgan and her siblings as a burden.

Such nonsense, she realised. Edna would never see her family as a burden—not in the way Morgan had worried they were. It was clear to her now, and she felt silly for not seeing it before.

'Gran—' Morgan started, but her grandmother interrupted.

'There's more.'

'More? How could I possibly survive more?'

'Funny,' Edna said with a glare in Morgan's direction. 'I thought… Well, I've always wanted to give you the house.'

Morgan blinked. 'Which house?'

'My house. I thought I'd bequeath it to you. But then I decided to move back, and the Abels decided to buy the estate…' Edna shook her head. 'There were several factors, really. Eventually I sold it.'

Morgan kept silent. She knew her grandmother. She knew there was more.

'But then I saw you here. How happy you are. I regretted it. So when that nice boy Gio came I asked him for the house back.'

'You asked…?' Morgan blew out a breath. 'What did he say?'

'Yes.'

She stopped walking. 'He said yes?'

Edna stopped, too. 'I told him it was for you, and that you'd worked for free to turn the estate into what it is now, and I said that I'd tell the community to make his life a living hell if he didn't sell it back to me.' Edna shrugged. 'He said yes.'

There was likely more to it than that. Gio was a businessman first and foremost—this was probably something he'd thought about strategically. But it didn't matter to Morgan.

'You're giving me the house? *Your* house?'

'Yes.'

Morgan shook her head. 'Gran, I can't—'

'Yes, you can.' Edna took both Morgan's hands in hers. 'I *want* you to have it. You deserve to be at peace. And I've never seen you more at peace than here, so I bought back the damn house for you.'

'Well, at least let me pay—'

'Morgan, I don't need the money. Your grandfather left me more than I expected, and I've been smart with it over the years. Not to mention that

I'm moving in with Stanley. The money I have left is more than enough to keep me going until I don't need it any more.'

She squeezed Morgan's hands before dropping them.

'Now, I believe it's time for me to get married. Let's go, dear. You'll make me late.'

Helplessly, Morgan followed her grandmother.

CHAPTER TWENTY

ELLIOTT HAD NEVER pictured his own wedding day. He'd never thought he'd get married. But since he was more inclined to such fanciful thoughts these days, he imagined this was the kind of wedding he'd want, too.

They'd set up the altar and the arch beneath the oak tree, and pinned flowers to every available space of the arch, creating the most stunning backdrop of white against the brown and green of the trees. There were white chairs in rows and rows, extending from the altar further into the garden. The flowering bushes added to the summery feel of the wedding, their bright colours a happy contrast to the simple white of the wedding décor. It was beautiful, and romantic, and the buzz from the rows and rows of guests—the only thing Elliott thought he might *not* want at his own wedding—added to the atmosphere of anticipation.

The groom stood at the altar, handsome in a navy-blue suit and not showing any nerves. But

then, Stanley was a steady sort of guy. The few
times Elliott had met him he'd been courteous,
patient. It was clear that he adored Edna, and that
she adored him, and Elliott imagined this was a
dream come true for both of them.

He wouldn't quite describe Stanley's son, the
famous videographer, in the same way. When
Gerald had walked into the garden he'd exclaimed
his pleasure. Then he'd barked instructions at his
team, begun filming, and now wherever he went
a nervous energy followed. Not his own, but the
energy of those around him, including whichever
guests he happened to be near.

Elliott was eager to see how that energy did
around Morgan. Her relentless cheer and no-non-
sense attitude were likely a match for Gerald.

Elliott caught himself smiling at that thought.
The moment he realised it, he stopped. His
brother was sitting next to him, towards the back
of the garden. What if Gio saw him *smiling?* At
nothing? No, that wouldn't do.

Unfortunately, that only made him think of
what Morgan would say if he ever told her what
had gone through his head. It made resisting a
smile harder, and he was grateful when music
began to play to indicate the entrance of the bridal
party.

Several bridesmaids came through first, one
of whom reminded him so much of Morgan that
Elliott did a doubletake. But when he did, he saw

that the woman wasn't as tall, with shorter hair dyed pink. Her features were different, too: her nose smaller, eyes bigger, mouth wider. She was obviously Morgan's sister, and the flower girl, who shared her mother's pink hair and big eyes, was Morgan's niece.

None of that mattered when he saw Morgan. She was wearing a dress in a colour that fell somewhere between purple and blue. It formed a V at her breasts, was cinched in at her waist, then fell sleekly down her legs, opening on one side to reveal a beautiful brown thigh. Shoes in the same colour as the dress adorned her feet, a silk strap hugging each calf and stopping right below her knee. Her hair was curled, tied in a ponytail at the nape of her neck, though some strands had broken free and were fluttering across her face.

He'd always thought her beautiful, but today she stunned the breath right out of him. And when she caught his eye, and gave him a coy half-smile, he thought he might never breathe easily again.

'Tell her,' his brother said at his side.

Elliott waited until Morgan was standing at the front with the rest of the bridesmaids before he asked, 'Tell her what?'

'That you love her.'

His head whipped to the side as Gio stood— along with everyone else—for the bride. It took him a moment longer to stand, but he did, and tried to focus on Edna. He couldn't. Though she looked beautiful and happy, he kept glancing at his brother, hoping for an explanation. And when it seemed clear he wouldn't get one, his eyes rested on Morgan.

He did love her. From the moment he'd seen her in front of her grandmother's house he'd been caught by her. Since then she'd tortured him, challenged him, teased him. She'd made him into a better man. He could easily see himself walking down the aisle right now, stopping in front of her and getting down on his knee.

The urge was so compelling that every muscle in his body clenched, as if to stop him from doing just that.

He was tense for the remainder of the wedding. At one point, his brother nudged him in the ribs.

'Relax,' he said under his breath. 'You're scaring the flower girl.'

Elliott looked at Morgan's niece who, despite the hundreds of other people in the garden, was somehow looking at him. When she saw him return her gaze she grinned, showing off a mouth full of various-sized teeth.

His lips curved. 'She's fine.'

His brother sighed, but didn't say anything.

Elliott made an effort to relax after that, for the sake of that stupid new and fragile bond between them. He didn't know what the rules were, so he wasn't sure what the implications would be if he ignored Gio. His heart thudded, and a familiar voice inside told him to throw it in. To stop caring.

It's too hard. You don't even know if it's going to work out.

But he ignored it. It took all his power, but he ignored it.

Because it *was* worth it.

Having someone to sit at his side at a wedding was worth it. Having that person tease him. Having that person be family. He'd shunned relationships out of fear, but never considered what that fear had cost him.

His eyes rested on Morgan and he knew what he had to do.

Except he wouldn't get the chance until later that night.

The celebrations began as soon as the ceremony had ended. Canapés and champagne were brought out as the couple had pictures taken, some alone, some with their guests. Every time he managed to get close to Morgan someone whisked her away, and he was left talking to a stranger, discussing something he didn't care about but trying not to show it because he was being polite.

Gio seemed to be having a ball, which was a confusing learning experience. Elliott hadn't realised his brother was so sociable. He'd only ever seen Gio working. It might be that Elliott just hadn't ever got to see Gio in his off time, but he had a feeling it was more that Gio didn't *get* much off time. He was beginning to think Gio's call for help hadn't only been for the company. Maybe Gio had called him as a show of trust— and in a first step to a better relationship and life.

Maybe Elliott would ask him.

Eventually, after hours and hours, the celebrations died down. There were still stragglers in the garden, drunk and happy—his brother included—while others had migrated to the beach. Elliott made sure Gio was okay, then began his search for Morgan. She was nowhere to be found, and nor were any of her family members, whom Elliott had met at various points during the wedding. His opinion of them had finally helped him understand Morgan's words about Gio.

'My feelings for your brother are entirely dependent on you.'

Her family seemed like nice enough people, but his judgement was based on Morgan's opinion of them. Since he wasn't sure what that was, he'd wait until he was before drawing any final conclusions.

In a last-ditch effort to find her, he went to the secret waterfall.

She was sitting on one of the rocks, staring at the water.

'Are you okay?' he asked, near enough that she could see him.

Her head whipped up, but she didn't seem surprised. She rested her chin on her knees.

'I think so.'

Slowly, he made his way to her side. She somehow managed to look even more beautiful than earlier. Her hair was untied now, falling in curls around her face. It reminded him of the last time they'd been at the waterfall together. But now, with the moon shining down on her, as if it had anointed her, he wanted to fall to his knees in worship.

Instead, he sat down, waiting for her to speak.

'It's trending,' she said quietly. 'Hashtag *romanceisland*. On social media. Gerald shot a video and posted it. A bunch of us reposted it, with the same hashtag, and then more people shared it because it's Penguin Island.' She smiled. 'We got *romanceisland* trending. It's a promising start.'

'It'll continue.'

'You sound awfully confident about that.'

'I am.'

'Why?'

'You,' he said simply. 'You did this. You won't fail.' He paused. 'I also know that Gio has invested a significant amount of money into marketing the estate. He'll make good use of this attention.'

'Isn't Gio just full of surprises?' she muttered under her breath.

'What does that mean?'

She didn't reply immediately. 'He sold my grandmother's house.'

Elliott's body tensed. 'I'll talk to him.'

'No,' she said, dropping to her knees. 'It's not like that. He sold it to *her*.'

'He…what?'

'He sold the house back to her for reasons that remain unclear but I'm sure are strategic. And she…' She blew out a breath. 'My grandmother gave the house to me.'

He stared at the waterfall, his brain working. Why hadn't Gio told him this? What was his plan here? He didn't think it was anything nefarious. Especially since apparently, Gio knew what Elliott's feelings for Morgan were. Had he done this for Elliott? And, if so, what was the end game?'

She squeezed his knee. 'It's a good thing.'

He looked down at her hand and took it. 'Is it?'

'I think so.' Her voice was shakier now, but she tightened her hold. 'I think… I think I'm going to move to the island.'

He didn't know how to reply. It didn't matter. She kept talking.

'I haven't been able to stop thinking about it since she told me this morning. But it's the right thing to do. I haven't talked to my family yet, but I'm going to—' she sounded resolute '—and I think some distance might help us all figure out how things will go from now on.' She looked at him. 'Am I...?' Her lashes fluttered. 'That's okay?'

He squeezed her hand tightly. 'If it's what you want, then it's more than okay. It's right.'

She let out a long breath. 'Why is making these decisions so hard?'

'You're changing your life,' he answered. 'That's hard.'

The waterfall was all they heard for a while, then she angled herself towards him. 'I saw you with your brother today. You two seem to be getting along well.'

'We are.' He allowed himself a small smile. 'It's...nice.'

She laughed. He wished he could bottle the sound and take it with him. Whenever he was having a bad day he'd shake it, uncork it, and let it shower over him. Give him the good feeling he had every time he heard it.

Good heavens, what was this woman *doing* to him? Turning him into a sap because he loved her...

'You what?'

He looked at her. Her eyes were wide, lips parted.

'What's wrong?' he asked.

'You just said I'm turning you into a sap because you love me.'

'I did not.'

'Yeah, you did. It was under your breath, and

quite frankly it didn't sound super-complimentary, but I heard it.'

So now he wasn't even in control of what he said.

He exhaled. 'It's true.'

She stared at him. Then she started laughing again. And if he'd thought she deserved worship before, watching her throw back her head now, exposing the long, smooth column of her throat, and hearing the infectious sound of her laughter would require sacrifice.

He supposed that was what love was. Sacrifice. Sacrificing his fears of rejection. Sacrificing the lonely life he'd created for himself and his feelings of unworthiness. He loved Morgan, so he would believe her when she told him he was worth her love. And because of that he would work every second to get to the point when he didn't have to believe her any more.

When he only had to believe himself.

Abruptly, the laughter stopped. She turned fully to him, her gaze searching. 'You love me?' she whispered.

He brought her hand to his lips. 'Yes.'

'I love you, too.'

His world shifted on its axis. But he didn't feel unsteady. The opposite, in fact. He felt as though things were finally right. As though his world, which he'd never been comfortable in, had settled.

'Thank you,' he managed to say through his emotions.

She laughed. 'You're not meant to thank me, Elliott. You're meant to say "I love you" back.'

'I already have.'

'So say it again.'

'I love you.'

Her lips spread into the sweetest smile and she leaned forward to give him the sweetest kiss. Slow, gentle, as if they had all the time in the world for the rest.

When she pulled back her eyes searched him. 'Are you going back?' she asked. 'To Cape Town?'

'I have to.' He frowned. 'I have to see my father.'

'He's not doing any better?'

'He's fine. But I have to see both my parents to…' He trailed off even as he felt his frown deepen. 'I suppose I have to face my ghosts.'

'Hmm…'

'But I'll be back,' he promised. 'For you.'

'No,' she said, shaking her head. 'You have to be back for *you*. You should want to live here, too. What about your job?'

He could hear her fear, so he pulled her closer, lowered his forehead to hers. 'I want this. You. A life together. I want us to base our businesses here. Fly out when we need to, but come back home to Penguin Island.'

He didn't give himself a chance to think about his next words.

'I want us to get married here. Maybe we'll have children, maybe we won't. But I want it all with you, Morgan. That's the choice I'm making because I trust us. Most importantly, I love you.'

She was kissing him before he'd finished, and he relished it. Poured his heart and soul into it.

And when she pulled away, she whispered, 'Yes… Yes, I'll marry you.'

If he'd known she'd take those words as a proposal perhaps he would have thought about it more. But as he smiled, as he kissed her again, he thought that sometimes things didn't have to be different to be perfect.

EPILOGUE

SIX MONTHS AFTER Edna's wedding Morgan finally moved into her grandmother's house. No—*her* house. It would be her permanent home, her base, though she was keeping her house in Cape Town. It was still a huge part of her, part of her history, and she needed somewhere to stay when she was in town for business. Which would be often.

It had taken months for her to figure out how her business would work with her move, and the result had been lots of travel. But that was fine with her. It meant she could go back to see her family as much as she needed to.

'After everything you've done for us, making this hard for you would be selfish.'

Those were the actual words her sister had said when she'd told her family about her plans. She'd decided not to tell them her feelings on everything—it would only hurt them, and what was the benefit in that?—only that she wanted to move to Penguin Island and wouldn't be there for them so much any more.

There had been a lot of back-and-forth: questions about why and how it would work with her job and her house. She'd been honest. Told them that the island had always felt more like home to her than Cape Town did.

When they'd seemed to accept that, she'd told them she was engaged, which had distracted them for much longer, and eventually, with her family all around, Hattie had told her that.

'After everything you've done for us, making this hard for you would be selfish.'

Morgan had teared up and looked at her grandmother, who had been smiling, and at her parents, who had been tearful themselves. She hadn't understood why, and had felt the familiar desire to soothe their discomfort in some way. But then her mother had nodded at her, her father had, too, and her grandmother had winked.

It was time for her to let go.

Apparently her family agreed.

Of course it helped that Elliott had been there the entire time. And that when he'd met with his family she had been there, too.

His parents had been kinder than she'd imagined, albeit uncompromising. But they'd given Elliott praise for what he'd done for the estate. She'd watched him as he'd heard the words he'd always wanted to hear. His expression hadn't changed, although he'd thanked his parents, and told them about the engagement. And that had been the end of it.

He'd told her afterwards that it hadn't felt the way he'd thought it would. But they hadn't been able to talk about it in detail because then they'd met up with Gio for dinner.

They'd wanted to tell Elliott's parents before telling his brother, keeping the news a secret until they'd left the island. When Gio heard he'd grinned widely, hit his brother on the back, kissed Morgan on the cheek and told her, 'Welcome to the family!'

Elliott's face had brightened, and Morgan had known he'd found the family he wanted. The one he deserved. She fully intended on expanding on that.

'Morgan?'

She whirled around. 'Elliott?'

She was jumping into his arms before he could say anything else. They'd been in touch every day of the last six months, seeing one another a couple of times here and there, but this had been their longest stretch without an in-person meeting. He'd been travelling for work, she'd had to get things ready for her move, and a month had passed. She hadn't expected him today, so jumping into his arms was the only reasonable reaction.

He caught her without missing a beat, spinning her around before setting her down on the ground. She clung to his waist, dug her face into his chest, and felt his warmth settle in her body. He was here, in her house, *their* home. They'd agreed he'd move his stuff in bit by bit, until he'd finalised his own business plans and could settle on the island on a more permanent basis.

In a couple of months they'd be married. And finally, their lives would begin in the place where their relationship had started.

'Good surprise?' he asked, pulling back far enough to see her face.

'Good surprise,' she agreed. 'You can help me unpack.'

He laughed, the vibration reverberating through her body. 'That wasn't what I had in mind.'

'Yeah, I'm sure.'

She rolled her eyes, but she was smiling as she turned in his arms. As he wrapped them around her she looked at the house.

And it hit her.

It didn't matter where they lived as long as they were together.

But it felt damn good to be together on Penguin Island.

* * * * *

If you enjoyed this story check out these other great reads from Therese Beharrie

Her Twin Baby Secret
Marrying His Runaway Heiress
His Princess by Christmas
Awakened by the CEO's Kiss

All available now!